Books By Lily Thomas

Giant Wars Series

Loving His Fire
Grounded By Love
Melted By Love
Wicked Flames of Desire

Galactic Courtship Series

Xacier's Prize
Claiming His Champion
Captivating the Doctor
Escaping the Hunt
Abducting the Ambassador
Wicked Prisoner
Seducing the Enemy
Cuff Me Now
Challenging the Arena
Dark Desires in Space
His Fallen Star
His Human Temptation
Racing Toward Desire
Zro'eq's Fallen Star
His Human Doctor
The Spy and The Alien
Her Desert Alien
Deceiving the Alien
Xacier's Queen
Taken by the Mobster
Seducing the Alien King

Ice Age Alphas

The Sabertooth's Promise
The Sabertooth's Mate
Direwolf's Desire
Direwolf's Heart

Seducing the Alien King

Lily Thomas

This book is a work of fiction. Names, characters, places and incidents either are products of the author's imagination or are used fictitiously. Any resemblance to actual events or locales or persons, living or dead, is entirely coincidental.

Cover created by SelfPubBookCovers.com/ Viergacht

www.lilythomasromance.com

ISBN: 9798476646600
ISBN: (ebook) B09CYR5CQL

Chapter 1

The room fell silent as Valeria digested the question that had been presented to her. The Earth government had offered her a generous sum of money to perform a mission that would be dangerous, probably life-threatening. There was no probably. Who was she joking? Most likely, she would never come back alive. The risk assessment showed about a sixty percent chance she would make it back with her life.

"Let me get this straight," Valeria kicked her long legs out in front of her as she leaned back in her chair and folded her arms across her chest, "you want me to pose as the Sri'thaen king's concubine?"

The woman seated in front of Valeria nodded her head. "I think you will find the money to be a good deal."

"Unless I wind up dead." A sixty percent chance she made it back? That was basically like flipping a coin.

The woman inclined her head as she pushed her glasses up her nose with a finger. "There is a great deal of risk, but I heard from a source you enjoy a good challenge, which is why we reached out to you. This will be the greatest challenge you'll ever face."

It was true. Valeria lived for the thrill of a good mission, whether it be stealing, killing, infiltrating, or just causing someone else a headache. She was the best at it, and other's misery caused her a great deal of joy.

"I haven't even heard of a Sri'thaen king before. Are you sure your intel is good?" Valeria unfolded her arms as she leaned forward in her seat suddenly as she studied the human woman in front of her.

"Our intel is faultless." The woman steepled her hands in front of her as she leaned over the desk a bit. "Almost no one knows there is a Sri'thaen king because he seems to be a well-hidden Sri'thaen secret."

"Why?"

The woman rolled her brown eyes as she leaned back in her chair. "We have no idea." The woman waved her hand in the air like she tried to swat a fly. "Perhaps they are worried someone might try to assassinate him, or maybe he is grotesque. We have absolutely no idea. The Sri'thaen council seems to make all decisions, so we aren't sure how much power the king wields."

"You just want me to gather information then?"

"If you think you can kill some higher-ups, like the council members or even the Sri'thaen king, and get away, we would prefer that. Causing a bit of chaos amongst them would be beneficial for the war, but gathering information is also a key part." The woman speared Valeria with her eyes. "The war is not going well for Earth. I won't lie. We are getting desperate. We've started something we might not be able to recover from."

Valeria didn't betray her emotions on her face, but inside, surprise pierced her. All Earth news segments portrayed the war as going well, and no need for any citizen to worry. Of course, Valeria didn't trust the government to speak the truth. Still, she didn't realize they were having any significant issues holding back the Sri'thaen forces.

"Double the credits." She might want to help her people, but she did have to pay for her lifestyle and food. If she died, she wanted those she left behind to be taken care of. She had lots of aunts, uncles, and cousins. She couldn't claim to be particularly close to any of them, though she did try to make family events. It helped that her aunt Margarita cooked the best tamales known to human kind.

The woman gasped before her eyes narrowed on Valeria. "Greedy, aren't you? I think one million credits is enough."

"Nope." Valeria stood up from her seat, acting like she was ready to leave the room. One million credits was definitely enough, but if she could get more, then why not? "Two million paid right now to my account, or I walk, and you can find someone else who enjoys the challenge just as much as I do with my success rate." Which would be difficult if not impossible.

The woman huffed and puffed as she glanced between Valeria and the pad in front of her. "Fine. Two million credits." Her fingers flew across the pad resting on the desk in a flurry of movement. "There. Check your accounts. The credits have been deposited." The words sharp with irritation.

Valeria turned her wrist toward her face and glanced at the screen on her watch. The two million credits were now hers. "I accept the job." If she died, her will would split the money between her family and her favorite charity. There was a planet that took in unwanted children and gave them a good start in life. Too many children were abandoned or orphaned. Space tended to be dangerous, and as more humans left Earth, more families faced the harsh reality that was space.

"Now," the woman rose from her seat and walked around her desk, the tips of her fingers brushing over the surface, "we have a slave ship waiting to take you to the Sri'thaen home world."

Valeria backed up, allowing the woman some room as she led Valeria out of the office.

The woman's eyes flickered over her. "And they'll put you in something more…" the woman waved a hand before saying, "provocative."

Valeria glanced down at her black cargo pants and dark hoodie with combat boots. She could see how this might not be considered sexy. Each baggy article of clothing hid her toned curves and concealed weapons.

"Come." The woman said as she shook her head. "We have a timetable to keep up."

Valeria chuffed in amusement. It didn't take much to rile this woman.

They walked briskly down a long corridor. After a few minutes, they arrived at a docking port on the military space station.

A mountain of a human man stood by the door decked out in some clothes which were in major need of a wash and some repair. He smiled at them, showing off pearly whites which looked strange in his grimy face. Streaks of grey and black ran over the skin of his face like he'd just finished repairing an engine.

"This will be your ride to the Sri'thaen home world." The woman nodded to the man. "This is

Antonio. He's been in the sex slave industry for about thirty years, so there's no reason for the Sri'thaen government to suspect him of working with us, and we've paid him very well for this mission."

Valeria didn't care who he was. She wouldn't trust him as far as she could throw him. Once they left this station, he could run with the money and do whatever he wanted, and she was about to be unarmed and under his control. It unnerved her.

"I hope you have some outfits because this," the woman motioned to Valeria, "is all she came in."

Valeria scowled at the woman's back. Just because she didn't dress sexy didn't mean she had nothing to offer.

"We have a lovely selection of dresses that are sure to highlight her attributes… assuming she has any." Antonio peered at her as if squinting would give him x-ray vision to see under her baggy clothes.

Her eyes narrowed on Antonio. "Someone must have thought I looked good, or I wouldn't have been hired."

"She's got bite!" Antonio laughed, then his lips fell flat as he pointed a meaty finger at her. "You'll want to make sure you don't put off a possible Sri'thaen buyer with that mouth. Some like a little sass, but most like docile females. It's the appeal of human women. They are weak and tiny compared to their alien buyers."

"I'll keep that in mind."

Antonio glanced at the digital watch on his wrist. "Time for us to get going. The Sri'thaens don't like it when we're late."

When Antonio turned to walked onto his ship,

Valeria followed after him. Here went nothing. Her mission was to act like a sex slave and hopefully draw the eye of the Sri'thaen king or someone of high rank in the Sri'thaen government. If that didn't happen, her mission would be over, and Valeria knew Earth would want their two million credits back.

"This is never going to work." Antonio shook his head sadly as his eyes followed Valeria's strut across the room.

"What?" She stopped short and placed her hands on her hips as she faced him. "Why isn't this going to work?"

"I'm known for selling sex slaves, but sex slaves know how to move their bodies, and you," he shook his head again, "have no idea how to move your body. It looks like there is a stick up your ass."

Valeria frowned. As much as she wanted to argue with him, she knew he spoke the truth. Instead, she sighed. "What can I do?"

Antonio rose from his seat and stood in front of her. "You need to remember those lovely hips of yours." He grabbed her wrists, moving her hands away from her hips. "And stop placing your hands there. A sex slave is alluring, not ready to do war with the universe."

Valeria rolled her eyes. "Then you show me."

"Better yet…" Antonio drifted off as he strode over to a communications panel and pressed a button. "Azia, do you mind coming up here?"

"Where are you?" A sultry voice asked from the panel.

"In the auditorium."

"I'll be there in a couple of minutes."

Then the line went quiet.

"Auditorium?" Valeria glanced around. The room was large sure, but it was in no way an auditorium.

"We call it the auditorium. It sounds better than calling it the initiation room." Antonio chuckled. "This is where all new sex slaves come to learn or show what they know. Auditorium seemed like a fitting name for it since each sex slave is an actor or actress in a way. He or she is ready to be whatever the client needs or wants."

Valeria shrugged. Whatever. Not like she cared.

The door to the room swooshed open, and in walked a drop-dead gorgeous Vrak'rir female. A sheer material covered her, well, barely covered her dark blue nipples and the triangle of black hair between her legs.

"You asked for me?"

The only word Valeria could describe her with was wow. The woman stunned with her grace and air of sexuality. If Antonio thought this pristine creature could teach her anything, then he would be disappointed. There was no way she would ever come close to matching this woman in beauty or talent when it came to enticing a man.

"We need help with this." Antonio motioned to Valeria.

"This?" Valeria snarled at him.

"I can see what you mean." Azia's dark eyes skimmed over Valeria.

If she had known this mission would require being insulted at every turn, she would have demanded three million credits rather than two.

"Perhaps she would feel and act sexier if she was dressed sexier?" Azia turned her gaze to Antonio. "We should make a visit to the wardrobe. We could even work on her makeup and hair." Azia sashayed her way over to Valeria and picked up one of her hands. "We should also work on these hands and nails. Her palms are a little calloused, and these nails. I don't think she's ever done anything with them."

"She's standing right here." Valeria grumped. Should have made it four million credits.

"I agree!" Antonio smiled. "We need to make her presentable for a king."

"A king?" Azia raised a dark eyebrow as she examined Valeria again. "I'm not sure even you can make that happen."

"So, we making me pretty, or are you guys going to bash my looks some more?"

"You'll need to teach her to curb her tongue if she wants a king." Azia tisked.

Antonio heaved a sigh like the weight of the universe hung on his shoulders. "One thing at a time, Azia. One thing at a time."

They ushered Valeria out of the auditorium, down a couple corridors of the sex slave ship, and then into a massive room. Racks of clothing lined the walls. More clothes than she'd seen in her life.

"With her tanned skin and long brunette hair, I think red would be a good color for her."

"No," Antonio shook his head, "she is to be offered to the Sri'thaen king. If she wears red, they will throw her into prison for causing a riot."

"Mmmm, yes. I heard something about Sri'thaen males being unable to handle the color red. Drives them insane with lust." Azia winked at Valeria. "If the king or any Sri'thaen chooses you, be sure to find a red outfit to wear for him one night."

"Thanks for the tip." Valeria would file it away for later use. Anything that helped her with her mission, she would eagerly stash.

"Now, let's get some of these outfits on and see what works for you." Antonio dove straight into the clothing, and Valeria knew it would be a long trip to Sri'thaen space.

Chapter 2

Antonio led his assortment of sex slaves out of the ship. Women from all sorts of species followed him, with Valeria being the only human out of the bunch. They hoped with no other humans, it might give her an edge on being chosen since human women were a favorite amongst alien species.

Each of the sex slaves wore what could only be described as belly dancer outfits. Valeria's outfit consisted of a purple top with little circles of gold metal that twinkled as she walked barefoot over the cool stone floor of the Sri'thaen building. The material cupped her breasts, using tension on her shoulder to lift her breasts high into the air. The top ended right under her breasts, leaving her toned abdomen exposed. Unlike her top, her loose-fitting pants of the same purple material was nearly see-through. Then there was the purple veil that obscured her face.

She felt like a trussed-up doll, but if this caught the eye of the Sri'thaen king, then she wouldn't argue with wearing it. Remembering her lessons on how to entice, she kept her hips loose and rolling.

Antonio followed a Sri'thaen guard through a doorway, and each of the women followed after. As she entered the room, Valeria took in the lush decorations. Colored pillows decorated chairs and benches where Sri'thaen men sat.

Through the purple veil, she couldn't get a

clear view of the men, but she figured the man in the middle front must be the king. He was tall, despite him sitting, and his clothing was slightly different from the other men in the room. She would presume he was the king and act accordingly.

Rocking her hips, Valeria did her best to draw his eyes to her wide hips and apple bottom butt. She did a lot of squats to earn herself this butt, and it rarely let her down.

All of the Sri'thaen men smiled in eagerness as the assorted alien women danced and twisted their bodies in front of them, except for one man.

Valeria's eyes widened as the Sri'thaen king yawned. Openly. He found this whole thing boring. How was she supposed to attract a man who didn't find any of them interesting? It didn't even look like he wanted to be here. His eyes drifted anywhere except the women.

There went the two million credits. Valeria was sure Earth would demand to have them back if she didn't kill any Sri'thaen officials or escape with some juicy intel to help Earth put an end to this war.

Stepping forward, Valeria raised her arms beside her, gracefully bending them this way and that as she twisted her body to the side. Then she arched slightly backward as she drew her waist forwards, doing slight circles. Those tiring lessons with Azia needed to pay off to make all her work worth it.

The Sri'thaen king's eyes glanced over her, but it was only a fleeting perusal.

Valeria kept a smile plastered on her face. Even though a veil covered her face from view, she didn't need him catching the hint of a frown. Azia had been clear during their lessons that a female face was more pleasant when it smiled.

One of the other women stepped forward in her light blue outfit, which contrasted sharply with her space black skin, and began to belly dance, attracting all the attention in the room.

Valeria wasn't familiar with belly dancing, but she knew how to move her body, and she figured she could mimic the woman beside her.

Rocking her hips side to side and then back and forth, she made the small of her back curve, pushing her stomach out and in. Then she raised her hands above her head and vigorously shook her hips as she spun around in a tight circle, causing the little metals circles to ring.

The Sri'thaen king's eyes moved to her, and she smiled broadly as his eyes moved to her waist.

That was right. He should pick her as his next concubine. Not only could she move her body while dancing, but she could move her body in bed as well. There were no complaints from past lovers. None at all. No matter how much Azia and Antonio scoffed and mocked her body.

She lowered one hand and crooked a finger at him, inviting him to her. He didn't take her up on the offer, but he tossed her a grin of appreciation.

Spurred on, Valeria raised her hands over her head and spun as she shook her hips. The little metal circles singing out in the room. As she came back around, she gaped at the empty seat in front of her.

Forgetting her dance routine, Valeria glanced around the room until she spotted the Sri'thaen king's back. He walked over to a door, which slid to the side, allowing him entrance, before it closed after him.

One of the Sri'thaen men walked over to Antonio. "It appears our king doesn't find any of your women to his liking. Here's something for your time." The Sri'thaen turned his attention to the pad in his hand, and Valeria assumed he sent some credits into Antonio's accounts.

"Well, time for us to go." Antonio turned to the women, ushering them out of the room as some Sri'thaen guards strode up to see them on their way off the Sri'thaen home world.

Valeria sidled up to Antonio as she whispered under her breath, "He didn't choose anyone."

Antonio glanced down at her with a raised brow. "Sometimes that happens. I have no control over who he does or doesn't choose. Maybe you simply weren't his type."

"Can you distract the guards as we walk back to the ship?"

Antonio shrugged. "I can't promise anything, but I will try."

"Whatever you can manage. I have a plan." Valeria said as she stepped to the back of the line.

The women walked down a corridor of white stone. The Sri'thaen building was beautiful. Valeria saw they had put a lot of work into it. Most societies moved from stone work to metal-based structures, but the Sri'thaens seemed to enjoy more organic architecture.

"Oh!" Antonio announced loudly.

Valeria ever so slightly tilted her head to glance over her shoulder to see Antonio snap his fingers high in the air as he turned to address the Sri'thaen guards.

"I forgot a pad back in the room." Antonio made a move to head back to the room they had left, forcing the guards to turn their backs on the women.

Antonio just gifted her with an opportunity like he promised.

Glancing about wildly, Valeria noted a door just a few steps away from her. Quickly, she darted over to it. Her shoeless feet didn't even make a whisper of noise. She held her hands to the metal circles on her top to keep them from clinking. As she walked up to the door, it slid to the side without a sound. Once on the other side, she paused. The door closed.

Waiting, she prepared herself for the Sri'thaen guards to barrel through the door, but when several minutes passed with no yells of alarm, she relaxed.

Now, Valeria needed to figure out what to do from here. She could sneak around and see what information there was to gather before getting the hell out of dodge. She was known for her uncanny ability to get out of sticky situations, so she wasn't too alarmed about being discovered. If it came down to it, she knew she could play the silly little sex slave looking to escape her captor's grasp.

Valeria took in the room she had dashed into. It was like one of those roman baths of old. Something she'd only seen photos of in a history class long ago.

A giant pool of water sprawled out in front of her with bubbles. Mounds upon mounds of bubbles and the perfumey air had her thinking it might be a giant bubble bath. Enormous white pillars of stone dotted the room, acting like they held the ceiling up, but she got the feeling they were merely decorative. Colorful pillows laid beside one side of the pool where there was a small sitting area with a low to the ground table.

The room spoke of money and power to Valeria. She easily imagined the Sri'thaen king coming here to bath every evening, and if she was correct, the sun over the Sri'thaen city would set soon.

A wicked smile spread across her face.

A new plan formed in her mind on how to get the Sri'thaen king to choose her to be one of his concubines.

Quickly, Valeria shed her veil and sexy outfit. She flung the outfit with a grimace. It hadn't done her any good in winning over the Sri'thaen king. All those stupid lessons for no reason. She would have had a better chance of attracting his attention in a black shirt and a pair of cargo pants.

Once she was stripped naked, she walked over to one side of the pool and saw some underwater stairs. Dipping a toe into the water, she smiled when she found it warm and pleasant. As she stepped deeper into the water, a sigh escaped her as she momentarily forgot where she was and why. The moment the water was waist-high, she pushed off the bottom and sent herself sailing through the water until she got to a depth where she was barely able to touch the bottom of the pool.

Now that Valeria swam among the bubbles, she realized how mountainous they were. She could easily hide among the perfumed bubbles. It was almost magical. If she survived this, perhaps some of her credits would go towards a bath like this.

It'd been years since she last enjoyed a bubble bath. Nowadays, she didn't have time. Not to mention that sonic showers were steadily taking over water showers. Water was weight in a spaceship, while sonic showers saved weight. Not only that, but her job kept her too busy to ever find and use a bathtub. She barely had time to eat between jobs, let alone time for relaxing, vacations, or bubble baths.

Valeria took a moment to let all the stresses of her life wash away as she laid back and floated on the water among the mountains of bubbles. It was only then that she saw the tiled design of the ceiling. Someone had painstakingly placed colored tiles on the ceiling to show a story.

A man stood among people with his arms outstretched. She didn't know anything about the story, but she guessed it was a portrayal of the Sri'thaen king overseeing his people like a father would look out for and protect his children.

A creaking noise from the other side of the room had Valeria shooting up as she sank into the water and peered around a mountain of bubbles.

A man stood on the other side of the room. A black and gold robe wrapped around his body, and even from this distance, she made out an impressively large frame. With a flick of a wrist, he sent the robe flittering to the tiled floor.

Valeria's mouth went dry.

Oh, stars.

It was the man she suspected of being the Sri'thaen king, and he was strikingly handsome. So handsome.

The ridges of his defined abs stood out, and

then there were his pecs. Mmmm. Her eyes drifted down the cords of muscles in his arms. Thank the universe! If this was the king, her mission would be one of pleasure! Which was preferred since she planned on sleeping with him to get closer to the officials of the Sri'thaen government. She might not have to pretend he was the best thing since sliced bread. He was the best thing since sliced bread.

When he strode towards the pool, she ducked further behind her mountain of bubbles. His first foot dunked into the water. Soon, he was chest high in the water. Suddenly, he dunked his head under the water and popped up a couple of feet away from her.

Valeria's breath caught in her chest. He was so close she could reach out and touch him, and he had no idea she was there. And now that they were both naked in the pool, she felt her nerves rising up inside her. This was the first time she would use her body for one of her missions, and her heart wouldn't stop thumping in her chest.

The Sri'thaen king tossed his head back as he ran his hands through his short black hair, sending droplets of water flying through the air.

He was drop-dead gorgeous. It was another reason her nerves acted up. As much as she believed in self-confidence and loving one's body, she worried he wouldn't like her, and she would be shipped off the planet the moment he discovered her.

As his hands dropped back under the water, she caught sight of his double-pointed ears. An image of her flicking her tongue over the tips crossed her mind. Woah. She had no idea where that erotic image had come from.

Valeria began to chicken out as she watched the well-muscled man in front of her. There was no way for her to predict his reaction when she announced her presence. He could hurt her or kill her with his bare hands. Or holler and have a guard kill her. She had no doubt there were guards positioned all around the palace.

He continued to wash himself. Valeria sank deeper into the water, until her mouth was underneath the surface, and her nose was just above it. Then she felt a tickle. A tickle in her nose.

No!

Squeezing her eyes shut, Valeria willed the sneeze away. She couldn't sneeze. No, no, no!

"Ah, choo!"

Chapter 3

The mountain of bubbles flew in every which direction with the force of Valeria's sneeze.

Valeria gasped as her hands came up to her face to cup her nose. Her eyes rose to see the Sri'thaen king staring directly at her. Her heart hit the bottom of the pool as she met his icy blue eyes.

"Who are you?" His voice snapped through the air like a whip.

"One of the… sex slaves that were brought to you earlier," Valeria answered as her pulse raced under her skin.

"I don't remember picking any of you." He said as he slowly walked towards her through the water.

Valeria backed up, trying to maintain the distance between them as she gauged his reaction. "You didn't."

"Did one of my councilors chose you for me?" He asked as he continued to prowl closer to her.

"No."

"Then how did you come to be in my bathing pool?"

Valeria's back bumped into the side of the pool.

The Sri'thaen king stopped a couple of feet away from her and folded his arms across his chest, causing his biceps to bulge. He cocked a dark eyebrow as he waited for her response.

"I figured you just hadn't a chance to make a proper decision." She flipped her wet, brown hair behind one shoulder. "You did leave before any of the women finished dancing."

"Somehow, I doubt your main motivation was to make sure I didn't go lonely tonight."

Valeria huffed. "Fine." She would play a different act then and hope he bought it. "Have you ever been on a sex slaver's ship?"

He shook his head.

"Well, it's not the most comfortable, and although our slaver isn't cruel, I can't emphasize how scary it is being sold off to an unknown buyer. I'd rather choose my purchaser."

"And you thought to choose me?" He began to slowly approach her again.

Sliding along the pool wall, Valeria moved towards the shallow end of the large roman style pool. "You are handsome." She shrugged one shoulder. "I'd prefer to be a handsome king's concubine than some slimy alien's on a trashy planet."

"Who said I was king?"

"You've got a kingly air about you." Valeria's eyes took him in as they continued to back up into more shallow water. It was hard to describe, but it was in the way he carried himself. His eyes never left hers and his shoulders were straight, never slumping. He knew his place in this world and knew others would respect him for it. "Aren't you the king?"

He shrugged a shoulder in response before he moved through the water in a flash of sudden movement. For such a well-muscled man, he sure knew how to move and move quickly. He pushed her down on the steps leading into the pool, so her upper half was exposed while her lower half stayed below the surface of the water.

Valeria stared up at him with wide eyes. His shoulders blocked out most of the ceiling above them, and those icy blue eyes stared down at her.

"You want to be mine?" He rested his body over hers until she felt his eager member pressing into one of her thighs.

Surprisingly, her body responded with a thrill of excitement that shot straight to the juncture of her thighs. Instead of using words, Valeria spread her thighs and wrapped them around his waist as she threaded her fingers into his short hair and tugged his face down for a kiss.

The king's lips were soft and strong. When she teased the tip of her tongue against the seam of his lips, they parted, allowing her access. She purred as she tasted… mint? Yes, his breath was slightly minty, and she loved it. He groaned above her, and she celebrated her success. If she pleased him, he might keep her.

His large hands roamed over her body. He started with her breasts, squeezing the soft flesh, almost as if weighing them. They fit so perfectly in his grasp. His palms rubbed against the stiff peaks of her nipples, and she gasped, her mouth breaking away from his.

The king sank lower until he captured a nipple with his teeth, nipping it lightly.

"Oh!" Valeria exclaimed as a flood of heat pooled between her thighs.

When he sucked her aching nipple into his mouth, her back arched. She didn't need to fake any sounds as pleasure seared through her. This mission was going very well so far.

With a growl, the king's hands wrapped around her waist. Breaking away from her nipple with a smack of his lips, he lifted her into the air until her butt landed on the edge of the pool.

He spread her thighs, her feet dangling into the water. Her pussy was right at eye level, and he stared greedily at her pink folds. "You still want me?"

"Oh, yes." Valeria purred. Even if this wasn't her mission, she would want him. Stars! He knew exactly how to stir her, and he was easy on the eyes. Maybe she should have paid Earth government to be sent on this mission.

Gripping her ankles, he yanked her forward until her bottom rested right on the edge, and then his face descended. Her breath caught in her chest. He blew out a hot rush of air right over her clit, and she jerked in surprise and excitement.

Her hands gripped his hair as he took her sensitive bud into his warm mouth, sucking on it. "Oh, my stars."

He growled against her flesh. Her head fell back, and she moaned loudly, the sound echoing off all the tile around them. Then he slipped a couple of fingers into her slick core, and she knew she wouldn't last long. As his fingers pumped in and out of her, his tongue lapped at her bud, swirling this way and that.

It had been a while since her last partner, and her body was hot and ready to go. Her hips jerked, and she came with a throaty moan. Her pussy clenched around his fingers, and her mind went black until the pleasure eased, and she released her hold on his hair.

The king pulled back, and when she opened her eyes, she found his icy blue gaze on hers. "You are responsive and come fast."

Valeria shook her head. "Not usually. I just haven't been pleasured for some time."

"Hmmm, perhaps you were right in hiding away."

A creak from across the room had them both gasping. Before she turned, the king dragged her into the water, placing his large frame in front of her, blocking her from view. She was about to ask what he was doing when she heard a voice call out, "The council is hoping to meet with you today, my king."

"Yes. Tell them I will be there soon."

"I will."

When the door closed with yet another creak, the king turned to face her. His blue eyes skimmed over her. "What is your name?"

"Valeria. And yours?"

"Akkon."

Valeria quirked an eyebrow.

"What?" A smile teased the corners of his mouth.

"I thought you might insist on me calling you, Your Majesty."

Akkon chuckled as he shook his head. "I get enough of that from other people. Now, as much as I would enjoy soaking in here with you some more, the council waits for me."

Valeria followed Akkon out of the pool, her hand held loosely in his as he guided her up the stairs. As she walked slightly behind him, her eyes watched the water drip off his body and somehow managed to stop herself from drooling all over the floor. Not only did Sri'thaens have double pointed ears, but they also had two dark lines of skin that ran from the base of their skull to the top of their butts along their spine.

"Here," Akkon bent and grabbed a towel off the floor. "I wasn't expecting company, so we will have to share."

"I can share." Valeria smiled up at him, not even needing to play a flustered and willing concubine. The moment she'd set eyes on him, she was game to be his. There'd been a moment of hesitation, but it seemed to be unnecessary.

"Hold your arms out," Akkon instructed her.

Her eyebrows nearly jumped off her face. "You aren't going to use it first?" She held her arms out, and he stepped forward with the towel. By the time he finished drying her off, the towel would be cold and damp.

"I can't pass up the chance to run my hands over your body." The corner of his mouth curved up in a wicked smile as he started with one of her hands and gently wiped the soft towel up her arm. Working his way up to her shoulder, he stood behind her. Then he draped the towel over her head, rubbing her hair dry, moving lower to dry the long strands of her hair.

"You were right."

Valeria blinked as he moved to dry off her back, butt, and then legs. "What are you talking about?"

"I was wrong to have skipped over you."

A smile broke across her face as she glanced over her shoulder to see him squatting behind her. "How were you to know I might be this amazing?"

His blue eyes looked up at her as he leaned in and placed a kiss to one of her buttocks. "Perhaps I should have every potential concubine join me in my bathing pool."

"Maybe you should." Valeria faced forward.

Akkon rose and walked around her. He raised the towel to her throat and dried her going down, taking time with her ample bosom. With the towel between them, he cupped her breasts, seeming to weigh the heavy orbs in his hands.

Valeria tipped her head up to meet his gaze, and she found him assessing her reaction. Did he think she would slap his hands and run away? She figured any good sex slave would stand here and do or take whatever her master wished. And it was easy since she found him attractive.

"Mmm, that feels good." She purred in her sexiest voice.

Akkon released his hold on her breasts and ran the towel down her abdomen and then to the juncture of her thighs. He bent down on his knees and slid a hand between her thighs.

"Open for me."

Valeria didn't hesitate to spread her thighs. Cool air swooped in and chilled her nether regions until he rubbed the soft fibers of the towel against her sensitive nub. A pleasured gasp escaped her, and Akkon rubbed her with slow deep strokes. The fabric felt so good against her, and her legs trembled as her already well-pleasured body prepared itself for another orgasm.

"Oh yeah." Valeria moaned as her fingers dug into his hair, steadying her trembling body.

"Does this feel good?" Akkon asked, his voice husky and deep, sending thrills of excitement running down her spine and straight to her sex.

"So good." She replied between pants. "Sooo good!"

It wasn't going to take much or long for her already excited body to orgasm again. Her fingers dug deeper into the black strands of his hair as she pulled on them lightly.

Akkon pulled the towel from her, but then something hot and wet replaced it. Glancing down with wide eyes, Valeria found Akkon's face pressed firmly against her mound of brown hair, his tongue licking over her clit in delicious strokes.

Her eyelids sank shut as her body shuddered around his face. "I'm coming." She gasped.

Akkon growled against her, sending sweet vibrations racing over her clit.

"Oh yeah, oh yeah, oh yeah." She panted as her hips bucked against his face, and she shattered. Her orgasm rolled through her until she slumped against his face, using his hair to tug his tongue away from her.

"I think you may have gotten me wet again." Valeria teased as she glanced down at him.

A broad smile spread across his face at her joke. "I still have the towel, if you need it."

Valeria couldn't stop the bark of laughter that escaped her as he bantered with her. She appreciated a man with a sense of humor, a man who could dish it back. "I think I'm good."

"If you are sure."

"I am."

Akkon picked the towel off the floor and wiped down the rest of her legs. Then he stood back up to his full height and held out the towel to her. "Your turn to dry me off."

"My pleasure." Valeria took the offered towel and eagerly wiped the fabric over his chiseled chest. His skin was nearly dry after all the time he'd spent wiping her off, but if he wanted her to dry him off, then she was all too happy to feign it.

Working her way down one arm, she raised an eyebrow at the size of his biceps. "Do you exercise a lot?"

"I do."

"What kind of exercise?" Valeria asked as she worked her way to his hand and then worked on his other arm.

"Hand to hand combat, weights, and I enjoying running."

"Running?" Valeria glanced up as she finished with his other arm and then squatted in front of him and began drying him from his feet up.

"We have many wonderful parks around the city. I find a morning run helps get my blood flowing and gives me extra energy for the day."

"I enjoy running as well."

"You are welcome to join me for my run tomorrow morning."

Valeria worked her way up his thighs to where his rigid member stood proudly from between his thighs. Before she could do anything about it, he held his hands down to her. "You don't want anything?" She slipped her hands into his, and he helped her to her feet, the towel landing at their feet.

"I don't think it will ever go down around you while you're naked. Even if I slaked my lust. No woman has stimulated me quite like this in a long while." Akkon released her hands and grabbed the towel off the floor, wrapping it around his waist before walking over to a wall where a robe hung on a hook. Grabbing it, he walked back over to her. "For you to wrap around yourself. Consider yourself accepted as my new concubine."

Yes!

Valeria figured she had to be in the minority when it came to wanting to be a concubine. Now she actually had a shot of getting close to him and any other higher-up officials he might mingle with. It was perfect.

Snatching the robe from him, she wrapped it tightly around herself and tied one of the fabric belts around her waist, holding it closed. It was a bit long on her, probably meant for Akkon's height rather than her short stature.

"Where to next?"

"Next, we get you settled in the room for concubines," Akkon said as he turned and led her towards the same door she'd entered through.

Disappointment flooded her, and she shoved it aside. She hadn't been with him long, but she enjoyed speaking with him, and now she was about to be introduced to the other concubines. They were sure to be her enemies. In any movie or book Valeria had read or watched, concubines were constantly vying for their master's attention. She figured these concubines would be no different.

They left the bathing room behind and walked down a long corridor before he drew up in front of a metal door.

"This will be where you stay."

"See you in the morning?"

"In the morning." Akkon picked up one of her hands and placed a gentle kiss on the back of her fingers, his eyes staring directly into hers.

A blush crept up her neck and cheeks. It appeared she'd found herself a spot, and not only that, he wanted to see her again.

Akkon dropped her hand, straightened, and strode down the hall. His long legs carried him far away from her, leaving her with the door in front of her. Turning back to the door, she pushed a button beside it, and it slid open.

Valeria stepped through the doorway and into a white stone room. Fabric draped down the decorative columns that ran between the floor and the ceiling, like in Akkon's bathing room. The purple and gold fabric added some color to what was a very white room.

"Who are you?"

Valeria's head snapped to her left, where she spotted a large group of women in a sitting area that was cut into the floor. It was laden with a ton of colorful pillows. The women were from different species and scantily clad. This had to be Akkon's concubines.

"Hi." Valeria waved a hand at the women. "I'm… I was bought by Akkon today."

"That ship left a long time ago." A woman with bright purple skin folded her arms across her ample bosom. A bosom that threatened to pop right out of her skimpy top.

"I suppose it did," Valeria confirmed as she turned her body to face the group of women.

"What could you have been doing for so long?" The woman's eyes narrowed as she skimmed Valeria up and down. "Did you take a bath?" Then the woman's eyes widened, and before Valeria could answer her questions, she said, "Did Akkon take you to his bathing room?"

Keeping her face straight, Valeria smiled inside her mind. She knew she should try to befriend the woman, but it was right there. One simple sentence, and she could irritate the shoes off the purple-skinned alien. "We had quite a lovely time in his bathing pool."

Most of the women gasped, and some even dropped their jaws.

"But… but… but," the purple woman blustered, seeming unable to come up with any other words.

"He hasn't taken any of us to his bathing pool." Another woman stood with a welcoming smile. Her exposed skin was dotted in cheetah-like spots, and her eyes… they were the eyes of a cat. Her black, oval pupils dilated against the yellow irises as her eyes skimmed over Valeria.

"Aren't you all his concubines?" Valeria asked as her eyes glided over the women. No wonder Akkon hadn't picked anyone off Antonio's ship. Akkon already had a good assortment of gorgeous women.

"We're supposed to be." Another woman said, this one a Daen'su. Her silver eyes filled with happiness and light like she had no cares in the universe.

"Here," another Daen'su scooted over on a pillowed bench and patted her vacated spot invitingly.

Valeria walked over, still wearing the robe Akkon had given her. At some point, she would need some real clothes, but for now, she didn't want to miss the opportunity to befriend the women she would live with. They might even know where she could get some clothes.

"Thanks." Valeria took a seat and glanced around at the women.

"So," the purple-skinned alien glanced her up and down, "what happened between you and Akkon?"

A blush threatened to creep up her face as she recalled all they'd done in the bathing pool. "Well, we pleasured each other." She shrugged as she looked around the other women.

"You must tell us more."

"Yes," another agreed, "I haven't been touched by a man in five months."

"Akkon hasn't been with you in five months?" Valeria raised an eyebrow. She figured he enjoyed one or more of the women every night. He looked like the kind of man who held plenty of stamina.

"He hasn't been with me since he bought me." The woman answered. "I'm Alvae." She held a closed fist over her heart. Valeria knew enough about the Daen'su to know the gesture was equivalent to a handshake.

"I'm Valeria." She held a closed fist to her heart, earning herself a smile from the two Daen'su sitting around her. At least she had won favor with these two with a simple gesture.

"I'm Sar." The other Daen'su offered her name.

"And I'm Fanka." The Dekkarian smiled, her yellow cat eyes dancing with interest.

Valeria turned to the other three women, but they simply glared at her, not offering their names.

"Ignore them." Fanka rolled her eyes. "They're bitter because Akkon hasn't paid any of us any attention since buying us."

"If he isn't sleeping with you, then why did he buy you?"

Sar shrugged. "We aren't sure. After he bought me, I've only seen him from a distance, never close enough to ask him anything, but he treats us well. We are fed, entertained, and allowed to go anywhere inside the palace and outside the palace with an escort for our safety."

"It's much better than where I came from." Alvae nodded her head, her long silver strands swaying around her shoulders. "I was skin and bones when I arrived." She pursed her lips. "Akkon took one look at me and purchased me. To say my slave ship owner was confused would be an understatement. He tried to sell Akkon any other woman, insisting he wouldn't be happy with me, but Akkon insisted on me… and then he never touched me."

Valeria frowned. These women made it sound like Akkon had saved them.

"Same for me, except I wasn't skin and bones. Instead, my entire body was covered in bruises from being beat by my slave ship owner." Fanka said.

"If he doesn't like the treatment of you all, why does he buy you? In the end, it gives the slavers money? It will only encourage them to continue selling. And abusing."

The purple-skinned alien snorted in the background, and Valeria chose to ignore the woman. They definitely weren't about to get chummy. She felt the bad vibes flowing off the other woman.

"I suppose," Sar said with a thoughtful tilt of her head, "that it's really all he can do unless he wants to start wars with every seller out there. It might be small and maybe doesn't result in anything other than giving us a better home, but…" Sar shrugged, "I can't fault him for rescuing me."

"Now, that isn't true for all of us," Fanka said as she curled her legs under her bottom. "Selde," she pointed over to the purple-skinned woman sitting among two others. "She was the first one, and she was bought by Akkon for use as a concubine."

Ah. That would explain why Selde didn't like Valeria. Valeria wasn't an abused sex slave Akkon had rescued out of the kindness of his heart, and she'd admitted to having some fun with him in his bathing pool. If Akkon showed Selde no interest, then that made Valeria competition.

Valeria glanced over at Selde to see her glaring.

Wanting to get away from Selde, Valeria asked, "Do you think there are any clothes I could borrow? I don't think I want to wear this robe for the rest of my life."

"Oh! Yes!" Sar bolted to her feet. "I think Fanka is about your size."

"I'd be happy to share some clothing with you." Fanka rose from her cushion and walked out of the lowered sitting area.

"Thank you."

"And we should help you with that hair." Alvae rose and followed the rest of the women as they guided Valeria through the decorative white pillars lining the room.

Valeria reached a hand up to her wet hair. "I think it will dry fine on its own."

"Not if you want to attract Akkon." Alvae shook her head with a dreamy sigh. "I must admit, I always hoped to turn his eye, but he's never glanced my way."

Valeria understood Alvae. Not only had he rescued most of these women, but he was an attractive man. More attractive than he should be. A twinge of worry built in her chest that she might not make it out of this mission with her heart intact. So far, he appeared attractive inside and out.

"Any idea why Selde and Akkon don't sleep together anymore?" Valeria asked. If she wanted to captivate the Sri'thaen king, then she needed to learn more about him. Like what he liked and disliked. If she needed to play a part to keep his attention on her, then she was more than willing. It wouldn't be the first time she'd played a part for the sake of a mission.

"I think he lost interest," Fanka said.

"I believe it was more than that," Alvae said.

"How so?"

Alvae pursed her lips as they stopped by a door that slid open when one of the women pressed a button beside it. "I think… correct me if you think I'm wrong," she addressed the other women before facing Valeria again, "She was too submissive and whiney for him. She went along with everything, and I think he grew bored of the relationship. It was nothing but sex, and even men want more than a physical relationship."

The other women nodded their heads in agreement.

"After Selde, I heard he took a few Sri'thaen lovers, but again, he seemed to lose interest, and I haven't heard of him taking anyone to bed of late."

Well, if Akkon wanted a headstrong woman, she would be the perfect match for him. There would be no pretending on her part. Plenty of ex-boyfriends ended their relationship with her, saying that they just couldn't handle her. As if her being a strong woman was the problem.

"Sooo," Valeria changed the subject back to the clothing inside the large closest, "which one of these can I wear?"

Each woman began speaking, and Valeria found it hard to concentrate on one voice as they tugged her into the closest. Deciding it better to let them lead, Valeria relaxed and enjoyed the moment of bonding with her fellow concubines.

Chapter 4

Akkon strode down the long, white, stone corridor on his way to pay for Valeria, the tempting human he couldn't get off his mind. Something about her appealed to him. Maybe it was her confidence.

A smile curved his lips.

Definitely her confidence. She'd waited in his bathing pool, naked, to inform him he'd made a mistake. No one told him he made a mistake. Even the Sri'thaen councilors handled him with care because although they had power, he had even more, and one misplaced word could be the end of their illustrious career.

After his most recent meeting with the councilors, he had contacted Captain Antonio to let him know one of his slaves had stayed behind.

As he entered a room, Captain Antonio turned, flanked by two Sri'thaen guards.

"I can't apologize enough." Antonio held out his clasped hands in a pleading gesture. "When you contacted me about the sex slave, I scarcely believed it. I'll let you know nothing like this has ever happened before."

Akkon raised a hand to stop Antonio from his blathering. "There is no need to apologize. I would like to purchase her from you."

"You… would like to purchase her?" Antonio blinked as though he didn't believe his ears.

Akkon understood the man's confusion. Valeria wasn't the average sex slave. Sex slaves tended to be on the timid and reserved side. Ready to please. They would never dare defy their owners and then try to stay with a potential buyer.

"I find her to be to my liking."

Antonio raised an eyebrow but inclined his head to one side. "She is the strongest-willed slave that ever stepped foot on my ship."

Akkon chuckled deep in his chest. "I could imagine."

"Sure you won't come to regret this?" Antonio asked.

Shaking his head, Akkon pulled out a pad and sent Antonio his running price for a sex slave. "I think she will bring excitement to my dull life."

Antonio shrugged. "You know how to contact me if you decide you need to sell her back."

"I know." Akkon agreed, but he didn't want to think about getting rid of her. Not when she was so new and exciting.

"Since I am here again, I wanted to personally thank you for allowing me safe travels through Sri'thaen space." Antonio bowed his head. "It was very magnanimous of you."

"I've known you before the war, and you treat your women well. I never once saw them underfed or covered in bruises, and with the skimpy outfits they wear, I would know."

Antonio bowed deeper. "Thank you. I try to be as fair to the women as I can. I've never once taken one who hasn't wanted this lifestyle."

Akkon nodded even though the human man

stared right at the floor. "Travel safe, Antonio."

He turned and left the room before Antonio could kiss his ass anymore. Enough was enough. People kissed his ass every day, and it wore thin quickly. What he needed in his life were people unafraid to tell him the truth of the matter, to help him improve himself. How could he better himself when no one found fault with him? He knew he hadn't been born perfect.

A little exercise would get out all this frustration and help him sleep later. Get Valeria off his mind too. Her tanned skin and dark brown hair still shone bright in his mind. Gods, she looked good in his bathing room. She'd been like a sun-kissed water goddess. He wouldn't lie. She had startled the pants off him when she sneezed. She made an impression, that was for sure.

It didn't take him long to find the combat training room within the palace. This was one of the many places where soldiers were trained.

"Your Majesty." A man strode forward the moment he entered. "What would you like to practice?"

"I think some hand to hand combat. I want someone equal to my skill." He pinned the other man with his gaze. "I want a man who won't hold back. I need a challenge." He needed something to take his mind off Valeria. None of his concubines had bothered him this much. His cock still raged inside his pants, and he wanted nothing more than to find her and finish what they started in the bath.

As Akkon entered one of the many arenas, he watched his opponent step into the padded area. The man opposing him was well built. He was shirtless, and Akkon nodded his head in approval. Hopefully, the man wasn't just muscle. He needed to know how to fight.

"Are you ready, my king?"

"Ready."

Akkon launched himself at the other man. The man dodged, and Akkon quickly side-stepped to avoid a punch towards his head. The other man's fist whizzed by his face, nearly brushing the tip of his nose. Ducking down, Akkon landed a solid blow to the man's side.

With a grunt, the man stepped back, and then they began circling each other. Each of them studied the other. Waiting for a weakness to creep through. When neither of them found a weakness to take advantage of, Akkon made the next move. Leaping forward, he dodged to the side at the last second, but the man predicted his move and landed a punch straight to Akkon's head.

He went down. Hard.

"Your Majesty!" The man rushed forward, as did several others.

Akkon's vision cleared to see the man's brows drawn over his eyes and a frantic beat to his pulse. "There is no need to fear. I asked for a man at the same skill level for this reason. I thought," he placed a hand behind his back and pushed himself up on the padded floor, "I could land you on your ass, and you showed me the error of my ways."

"Still, Your Majesty. I apologize. I shouldn't have punched you so hard." The man offered him a hand, and Akkon accepted it. Once pulled to his feet, he raised a hand to his head.

"Another round."

"Your Majesty." The man looked uncomfortable, even looking to the gathered crowd around them for help.

"I said another round." Akkon pointed a finger at the man. "And now that I know your skill, you best not hold back because then I will be angry."

Chapter 5

Valeria sat at one of the vanities in the concubine room the next morning. Spread out before her were so many bottles and containers, and she had no idea what they were and how to use them. Choosing one at random, she lifted it and fingered the design on the bottle. It resembled the head of some kind of animal, and she assumed it was an animal here on the Sri'thaen home world.

"What are you doing?"

Valeria turned to see Sar standing beside her. "This may surprise you, but I have no idea what any of these bottles are for."

Sar's eyes widened. "None?"

Valeria shrugged. "Before becoming a sex slave, I wasn't raised wearing dresses or makeup. The most I've done with my hair is put it in a ponytail or a bun. And maybe a dress for my quinceañera."

"What is a kins..." Sar trailed off as she struggled with the unfamiliar word.

"It's a celebration of a girl turning fifteen."

"Do all humans celebrate this birthday?"

"No," Valeria shook her head, "humans have lots of cultures and lots of parties and celebrations."

"Oh. Very interesting. I would love to hear more about it later."

"Yeah, whatever you want to know. I'm pretty much an open book. I must be the least feminine concubine the king has chosen."

"Maybe this is a reason why Akkon has shown an interest in you," Sar said.

"You think I interest him?"

"Oh, yes," Sar said as she tugged the bottle out of Valeria's hands. "This, by the way, is a bottle of perfume, but I don't think the scent will entice Akkon."

"I trust you," Valeria said, honestly believing Sar would never do anything harmful to her. She trusted her gut when it came to people, and she found no reason not to trust it now.

"That means a lot to me." Sar smiled at her in the mirror on the vanity. "Now, let's get you dolled up."

"Umm, actually," Valeria held up a hand, "I think Akkon might ask me to go for a run this morning, so maybe no makeup. Otherwise, I might look like I'm melting when I sweat."

Sar laughed, a good throaty laugh. "It would be funny to see his face as you melt in front of him."

Valeria laughed as she imagined it also. "And as you said, maybe he likes me because I am different than other women he's known. In which case, he might prefer me without makeup."

"True." Sar nodded her head. "How about a braid for your hair?" She tilted her head to the side as she lifted Valeria's hair and studied it in the mirror. "It will be pretty but easy to manage while running."

"I think a braid would work."

"Helping her to be beautiful?"

Sar and Valeria turned to see Selde standing

nearby, leaning against one of the many white pillars. Her purple skin standing out in stark contrast.

"She is beautiful." Sar defended Valeria without pause.

"She's just a human with boring brown hair and eyes." Selde's eyes raked up and down Valeria. "She's short and too fit. Nothing about her is womanly. There are no curves for a man to appreciate and enjoy."

"If you don't have anything nice to say, then leave Selde." Sar growled.

"If the truth bothers her, then maybe she should leave."

"Eh, just ignore her," Valeria said as she faced the mirror again. She didn't have enough time in the day to deal with someone like Selde.

Sar frowned but did as Valeria suggested. "I think we have some pants and shirts in the closet that would be good for running."

"Once you finish braiding my hair, I'll go sift through the clothing."

"I'll grab you a pair of workout clothes!" Fanka said as she raced by from out of nowhere.

"What?" Valeria glanced around the room. "Did you know she was nearby?"

Sar shook her head. "Fanka moves so silently. I don't normally know she's around until she announces her presence. I think it has to do with her species. Dekkarians are known as good hunters, and a hunter can't announce their presence to their prey. I believe they come from a jungle planet if I'm not mistaken."

Valeria would have to be careful of Fanka then. She didn't need the woman hearing or seeing something that would blow her cover. Not when she was so close to the king.

"Didn't the king promise a morning run with you?" Selde asked from where she leaned.

Valeria and Sar ignored her.

"Morning is almost passed, and he hasn't sent for you. Maybe he got busy, or maybe he wasn't as interested as you thought."

"He is a king," Valeria replied without even glancing over at Selde. "If he gets busy or forgets, I won't hold it against him."

Sar smiled at her in the mirror. "That is a good attitude."

"I think so. When it comes to building a relationship, you can't get upset at every little thing. Sometimes you need to go with the flow."

Selde huffed, and when Valeria glanced over, she found the woman gone.

"Guess she doesn't agree with me." Valeria rolled her eyes.

"I suppose not."

"I found the perfect color!" Fanka announced as she strode over with purple workout clothes draped across her arms. "This will go so well with your dark brunette hair and eyes." She held the fabric up to Valeria's now braided hair.

"Thanks!" Valeria reached back and took the clothes. As she stood, she asked, "Do you guys mind if I change right here?" She wasn't shy when it came to nudity, but she wanted to be respectful of the other women in the room, or at least respectful of the women she liked.

"We don't mind," Sar said as she and Fanka turned, giving Valeria a little bit of privacy.

Valeria quickly shed her clothing and then slipped on the tight-fitting workout clothes. "They fit like a second skin. I hope the Sri'thaens have no issue with such tight clothing."

Sar and Fanka spun back around.

"I don't think they are prudes. The only rule I know of is you are not allowed to wear read outside of a bedroom with your partner. Red causes male Sri'thaens to lose their minds. If you wore it in public, you could cause a riot, or worse."

"I heard about this." Valeria cocked her hip against the edge of the vanity table. "Any more you can tell me about it?"

Sar glanced to Fanka, who shrugged. "I don't think we have much more to pass along. Sri'thaen males simply want to fuck any woman who dresses in red. Now," she held up a hand, "I have heard males who are committed to a woman may not be as affected as those who are single or having relationship issues."

"So, a guy who is married is less likely to be attracted to a woman wearing red?"

"Correct." Sar nodded her head sharply.

"Valeria!"

Valeria straightened and turned to see a Sri'thaen male on the other side of the room.

"Yes?"

"You are to come with me. The king has requested your presence."

"Have fun." Fanka and Sar said in unison.

Chapter 6

When Valeria set eyes on Akkon, her heart nearly stopped in her chest. The man was definitely sex on a stick. He wore no shirt, white pants, and running shoes. It pleased her to see they would indeed be running this morning. A stretch of her legs was exactly what she needed.

"Good morning." She raised a hand and waved.

The guard beside her growled. "Good morning, Your Majesty, is how you should address him."

Valeria rolled her eyes. When they were close enough, she swept into a deep bow and said dutifully, "Good morning, Your Majesty." When she straightened, she found Akkon frowning at her. "What? Was the bow too much?" She glanced between Akkon and the guard.

"I thought you knew to call me Akkon."

"Well, this guy over here," she hitched a thumb at the guard, "growled none too politely that I needed to attach Your Majesty to the end of my sentence."

Akkon turned his ice-blue gaze to the guard. "She is to call me Akkon. I never want to hear Your Majesty out of her mouth. Too many people already say it."

"Ready for our run?" Valeria threw an arm

over her head, grabbed her elbow, and stretched out her arm before repeating the process with the other.

"A leisurely jog through the palace gardens?"

"Yeah, I can do leisurely." She bent over at the waist, reaching for her toes. If she didn't do some light stretching, she knew her muscles would complain later.

"Avert your eyes!" Akkon barked.

"What?" Valerie straightened like a whip. She hadn't thought she was looking anywhere inappropriate. Then she saw his eyes narrowed behind her. Turning just her head, she found the guard behind her. Oh. He must have checked out her ass. In an attempt to spare the guard, she rushed over to Akkon, grabbing his hand. "I'm ready for our run. You leading the way?"

Akkon took off, and she found a leisurely pace for him was a dash for her. Stars. The man was tall and his legs long. He ate up the ground with no effort. But as she was always up for a challenge and never one to complain, she kept up. It was a struggle, but she kept up.

"So, why all the concubines?"

"Huh?"

"Why all the concubines?" Valeria asked again. "When I spoke to them, they said you hadn't slept with any of them for years, and some of them never."

Akkon glanced over at her. His blue eyes searched her face as if he'd find clues there. "Why do you care what I do with my concubines?"

"I don't." Valeria shrugged a shoulder, and she pretended not to notice when he slowed his pace a little, allowing her to keep up easier.

"Then why ask?"

"Just curious why you would collect so many attractive women and not bother to bring them to your bed." It seemed a waste to her. Some of the women were even attracted to him.

"Perhaps I discovered that beauty wasn't enough to keep my attention."

"In bed? What more do you need in bed?" Valeria was serious. Did he need stimulating conversation while getting off? Because he wasn't going to find stimulating conversation with her in bed. Nope. All he would get was oh, baby, or do that again, or yeah, that's the spot.

"I needed more outside of bed."

"Ah, so really, you were looking not only for a concubine but maybe even a friend." Or maybe the guy needed a wife. Someone who stimulated him in bed and in conversation while standing by his side.

Akkon chuckled as they rounded a corner in the path. A beautiful garden of flowers waved in the light breeze, and Valeria smiled at them. She loved flowers. They had a way of making the worst situation feel better. In the hospital? Flowers. Break up? Flowers. At a funeral? Flowers. They made everything cheery and bright.

"I don't think I looked for a friend amongst the concubines. I have those. I want a woman I can bring with me to functions, who can talk about more than clothing and makeup. I need a woman who can help me lead my people."

"Sounds like you're searching for a queen," Valeria said before regulating her breathes through her nose. The run would really do one on her tonight. Maybe she could take a soak in a hot tub to prevent achy muscles.

Akkon fell silent, and she assumed he digested her comment.

They ran for several more minutes, and Valeria took the moment of quiet and enjoyed the sounds of birds and other animals she couldn't name. The sounds were nice. Most of her missions were in space on space stations or ships. Rarely did she get a chance to travel to a planet.

After about an hour of running around the extensive palace gardens, Akkon led them over to a small white gazebo. Pulling up in front of it, they both stretched once more, and then he led her up the couple of steps. She spotted a selection of food laid out on a low table. Two pillows laid on the ground, and she knew those would be their chairs.

"Did you set this up?"

He nodded.

It almost seemed… romantic.

Taking a seat, Valeria waited for him to sit before snatching a tasty looking pastry. When she bit into the flaky morsel, a fruity jam oozed out. "Mmmm, what fruit is this?"

"A *jab jab* berry."

"Never heard of it before."

"I would be surprised. They are only cultivated for the palace and not allowed to be sold anywhere else."

"Then I've probably never had one before." Valeria popped the last bite into her mouth. "Amazed the Daen'su haven't found a way to smuggle it off the planet and sell it on the black market. If any species could, it would be them."

Akkon shook his head as he selected a sweet treat. "Our home world is too guarded. Barely anyone is allowed in our solar system."

"You know," Valeria took another of the *jab jab* pastries, "I wondered why you allowed Antonio, a human, to come and leave without killing him or jailing him. Or even myself." She pointed to her chest. "With the war between our people, I thought your mission was to wipe out every single human."

The smile slipped from Akkon's face at the serious turn of their conversation. "As much as some of the councilors would like to kill Antonio when he visits, I have issued him a pardon."

Valeria leaned back. "So, the councilors have more power than you?"

Akkon growled low in his throat. "I don't wish to ruin our day with talk of the war or the councilors."

Valeria inclined her head to him when he pinned her with those piercing blue eyes. "As you wish." She held up another sweet treat, "Tell me about this one." Her mission wasn't to rush everything in a few days. She accepted it, knowing it might take her months, maybe even a year. Although, she did hope it wouldn't take that long.

The smile returned to his face as he began describing the food laid out before them on gold and silver plates and bowls. It was the most elegant picnic in a garden she'd ever had. It was the first picnic she'd ever had.

When presented with another opportunity, Valeria would try again to discuss the councilors and how much power he really held among his own people. For now, she would sit back and enjoy the pampered life of a concubine.

"Your Majesty."

Valeria glanced up and found a Sri'thaen male in a deep bow. His massive frame covered in black robes.

"You may rise," Akkon said in a dismissive tone.

When the man straightened, his eyes focused on Valeria, and he snarled. "A human. Really, Your Majesty? I heard the rumor, but I figured it must be wrong. What kind of message do we send to our people when you have a human as one of your concubines?"

Akkon snarled right back. "Watch your tongue, Zohx. I may not be able to rid myself of you, but know your place."

Zohx's brown eyes danced with gold flecks as he glared at Valeria for a few more seconds before giving his full attention to Akkon. "Rakshasas Sa'ri and Adira will be arriving to the palace later today. They bring news from the front lines."

"Have they passed along anything?"

Zohx's eyes slid to her. "In front of the human?"

Valeria snorted.

Akkon glanced between her and Zohx. "You should be more respectful of the human, Zohx. As my concubine, she has almost as much power as you inside this palace."

She smirked when she saw Zohx's jaw clench. The man hated her. Simply because she was human, and although she knew it would be a dangerous game, she felt the temptation to annoy him further if given the chance. She loved playing dangerous games. Got her blood flowing. Kept her on her toes. It might kill her someday, but at least she'd have fun till the very end.

"We've lost a couple of battles with the Kellian warships near the Sion system," Zohx informed Akkon.

"The Kellians have not backed down from their stance?"

"No," Zohx shook his head. "Ever since Xacier mated a human, he's made it his mission to defend Earth like it's his home world. The council has voted to take the fight to the Kellians as well. We need to prove to them we won't stand by and let them dictate to us."

Akkon nodded. "Let me know when Rak and Adira arrive. I would like to hear their perspective on the front lines."

"I will." Zohx bowed before leaving them.

"So, please ignore my ignorance, but he," Valeria pointed at Zohx's receding back, "just made it sound like the council made a decision without you."

Akkon picked up a berry and popped it into his mouth. "They have done this since I was a child."

"The council helped you while you were a child?" Valeria was missing some details here. If Akkon was king, then his father and mother should have been queen and king while he was younger.

"My parents both passed in a shuttle accident when I was very young. I was too young to take the throne and lead my people. I could barely use the restroom without help, I was so young."

"They ruled in your stead then." Valeria kicked out her legs, and Akkon captured one of her feet, peeling her shoe off, and began massaging her foot through her sock. "My feet are probably stinky." She curled her lip.

Akkon shrugged. "I don't smell anything."

"Oooh." She let her head fall back as he worked on the sole of her foot with a couple of thumbs. Why was she trying to convince him not to rub her feet? "Did you take back power when you were old enough to rule on your own?"

She watched Akkon's expressions through slitted eyes, not wanting him to know he was being watched.

"They've always been there to guide me."

"Guiding you is one thing, but it sounds like they just made a decision without you. Did you even sign off on this war?"

When his brow furrowed, she knew the answer. He had not been the one to decide on war. The council had.

"Can I be frank with you?"

"Frank?"

"Can I be one hundred percent honest with you without you threatening to chop my head off?" Valeria opened her eyes and met his gaze.

"Please."

"It sounds like you have little to no power. It sounds like and looks like the council is running in your stead and only keeping you in the loop as a courtesy. It should be the other way around. Sure, they can advise, but you should have the power to say yes or no."

When Akkon glanced away, she knew he thought about her words. She would let it simmer there for a bit and hope he realized she was right. Maybe she could twist her mission a bit. She was sent here to gather intel and maybe cause a little chaos in the form of one or more assassinations. Maybe she could cause chaos by helping their king find his voice and taking back power. To her, Akkon seemed less an enemy to Earth than the council.

Chapter 7

Embarrassment seared through Akkon. White hot and painful. Valeria had been here for barely a day, and she already saw so much more than others. As much as he wished he could argue with her and say he was more involved in the decisions about his people, he knew he couldn't honestly say anything.

The council had basically raised him and taught him to trust their decisions. When they needed him, they called him in. Otherwise, they ran the Sri'thaen government, and he played the rich spoiled king. It wasn't that he wasn't interested. He simply didn't know how to go about inserting himself back into a position of power. And before Valeria questioned him, it hadn't bothered him.

"What would you think," Valeria sat up and laid a hand on his bicep, "about attending a council meeting or whatever you call them randomly?"

Akkon studied her. "To show my interest in the running of my people."

Valeria shrugged a shoulder. "Only if you are truly interested."

"I am. Very much so. I love my people, and I want them to know I only wish the best for them."

"I think there's only one way to prove that."

He waved her on. This was the first time he'd ever heard anyone encourage him to take back power and his throne, and he wanted to hear more.

"Start attending the meetings. Make your voice known. If you can overrule decisions the council makes that you don't believe benefit your people, then overrule them. Show them you aren't just a figure head. Show them you can be a king like your father and his father before him."

Akkon shook his head. "Did the gods send you to help me find my voice?"

Valeria tossed her head back and laughed. It was light and musical. A smile broke across his face as he watched the fascinating human. She had been right to insist on him purchasing her. His life would never be the same. He knew this. Felt it in his bones. She would be the woman who shook his world and showed him the way.

"Do you want to eat anymore, or would you be up for a walk around the gardens?" She asked.

Snatching a couple more pastries, he rose and offered her a hand. "If you insist, I suppose I can go for a stroll in the gardens."

Valeria slipped her tiny hand into his, but he felt the strength in her grasp. Heck, he'd seen her strength and endurance while running. Instead of complaining about his long strides, she strove to keep up with him. He pulled her to her feet and then guided them out of the gazebo and into the extensive gardens. She was the kind of woman he'd always fantasized for himself.

"A kiss before our walk?" Akkon asked as he pulled her into his chest. Her mouth popped open on a surprised gasp and then curled into a smile as she leaned her head back to gaze up at him.

"I think I could be persuaded." Valeria purred.

Leaning down, he captured her soft lips. His tongue ran along the seam of her lips, and when she opened, he explored her mouth. He dueled with her tongue for a bit before pulling back. "Tastes like *jab jab* berries."

She laughed and slapped at his bare chest playfully. "As long as you like the taste of *jab jab* berries."

"I do." He laughed as he winked down at her. "Tastes even better from your lips."

Valeria rolled her beautiful brown eyes. They were so dark, almost black, except he saw some lighter streaks in her irises in the light. "You are such a flirt."

"Not normally," Akkon admitted. As a king, he didn't need to flirt or court women. They were more than happy to fling themselves at him. He had no practice flirting and wasn't sure he would know what it was even if it bit him in the ass.

Pulling away, Valeria led him deeper into the gardens, and he followed like a bug attracted to the light. Nothing could tear his eyes from her. He followed her as she sniffed and ooo'd and ah'd her way around the gardens. She would bend now and then, lift a flower to her nose, and sniff it like she'd never smelled anything better.

When a *girk* flew over to a flower, she gasped.

"What is this?" Valeria pointed to the very common pollinator.

"It is a *girk*."

"It looks like a flying pink frog." She stared in fascination as its long tongue flicked out, collecting nectar from the flower before rolling back into its mouth. Then it buzzed off to the next flower. "I have never seen anything so bizarre and cute."

"Cute? A *girk*?" Akkon looked at the fat, pink creature as it flew from flower to flower. When a second flew into view, Valeria nearly melted as she held up her hands to her face and ah'd over the thing. He'd never thought of them as anything but an animal, and seeing Valeria's reactions to it made him take a step back and really look at the creature. He supposed with the large green eyes and pink belly it might be considered cute.

"Do you think it would be okay if you took me to see the council chamber?" Valeria asked as she finally ripped herself away from the *girks*.

"Okay?"

Valeria cocked her head to the side as her brown eyes danced with amusement. "I think it would be fun to see the council chamber." When he folded his arms in front of his chest as he raised one eyebrow, she explained further. "I think it would be fun to see it. Imagine, I could be the first and only human to enter the chamber."

"Would you be surprised to hear you wouldn't be the first human inside the chamber?"

Valeria's eyes widened. "I am surprised, but I think you understand what I'm saying. Not many humans get the chance. I'm a human who is living and breathing on the Sri'thaen home world. I should experience everything I can."

"To answer your question, it would not be a problem. I can take you there. As king, who would stand in my way?"

"So, we should get cleaned up and then head over there?"

Akkon smiled. "I think I know the perfect place for us to get cleaned." Eagerly, like a young man, he grabbed her hand and led her from the gardens back to where they first truly met. His bathing room.

"Do all Sri'thaen's have bathing rooms like this in their homes?" Valeria asked as she tipped her head back and admired the ceiling.

He followed her gaze. "No."

"Not even the Sri'thaen nobles?"

"Perhaps, but your question referred to all. I'm sure not all would spend money on a bathing room as extravagant. Even I wouldn't have spent the money, but it was built several generations ago by a king with not only a queen but nearly a hundred concubines."

Valeria whistled low. "Damn."

"Damn, indeed." Akkon agreed. He couldn't imagine maintaining so many women. How a man created a relationship with each and every single one of them puzzled him. What was the point to so many women? It wasn't like a man could speak to every single one of them in a day. Even his cock agreed that was too many women.

"Don't intend to build up your little harem?"

When he glanced over at her, he found her half-naked. How had he not noticed? The bathing room was humid, and he wanted nothing more than to dive into the water. Apparently, neither could she. "No. I don't think I need any more women."

"I've heard some interesting things from the other women," Valeria said as she peeled off those tight pants.

He found himself unable to look away as she descended the bath steps and into the water. Her toned legs seemed to go on forever as she entered the warm water.

"Oh, this feels so good." She purred right before she dove under the water and then popped up a few feet away. She turned with a smile on her lips. "I'm so happy your great-great-great-great grandfather built this."

"Add in a couple more greats, but yes, I have enjoyed this as well. My father wasn't known to use it, and I have no idea why not." Akkon shed his clothing and was pleased to see Valeria ogling him openly. He had no idea why, but she felt refreshing and new. She questioned and challenged everything around her. She wasn't fearful of his position and power. Instead, she openly criticized how he allowed the councilors to run the lives of his people. She was right, though. He should be more a part of the running of his people.

Not bothering with the steps that led into the bathing water, Akkon strode over to the deep end and dove into the water, throwing his hands in front of his head.

Valeria watched Akkon's massive frame dive into the water with a grace she hardly believed possible. The man rippled with muscle, yet he moved with the grace of a large cat. The water enveloped him, and she waited amongst the massive mountains of fragrant bubbles for him to emerge.

When long seconds passed, she spun around in the water. How long could he hold his breath?

Unless he'd hit his head and was passed out on the bottom? A trickle of worry pierced her, which she squashed. If the king killed himself, it would be a mission complete. Easier than she ever could have imagined. Yet, something in her rebelled at the idea. He wasn't some cruel Sri'thaen king. He saved vulnerable women the best way he could.

Hands wrapped around her waist and lifted her into the air. Akkon's smiling face emerged from the water, water droplets flying every which way.

"Akkon!" Valeria gasped as her hands came down, clenching his shoulders. "I thought you may have bonked your head and were drowning."

"I'm sorry to have worried you." He drew her back into the water and against his chest. "But the view from under the water was… magnificent."

Valeria tossed her head back and laughed to the ceiling. His words were so unexpected. "I'll have to take your word for it." Her hands clasped his face, and she leaned up, planting her lips against his. He groaned against her as he leaned into her kiss. Her hands worked their way into his hair, and she reveled in the moment. This king was impossible. Impossible to resist. Maybe this mission would be harder than she previously thought. If she wasn't careful, she might just end up liking the man. So far, he had been fun and funny to be around. They talked so easily. And then there were his looks. Stars! The man was perfect.

Akkon's hands landed on her ass, drawing her up, and she immediately wrapped her legs around his waist. His erection pressed against her pussy lips, and she felt it throb with his desire. Striding forward, through the water, Akkon pressed her up against the wall of the bathing pool.

She nipped at one of his lips, and he growled, thrusting his length against her lips. The friction of his length rubbing up against her clit had her jerking her hips in response. His hands roamed across the bottoms of her thighs, and then he rubbed them over her sides. Water lapped at the edge of the pool as they thrust against each other.

As his length moved over her clit, she gasped as pleasure rocked through her. Did he plan on getting her off by just rubbing his length against her? On one hand, it was erotic like no other. On the other, she really wanted his length inside her.

"Akkon." She begged as her hips bucked against him again.

"What do you want, Valeria?"

"I want to feel you inside me." She wanted to feel his length stretch her until she couldn't take anymore. She felt his throbbing shaft and knew it would be tight but feel so perfect.

His hand slipped between their bodies, and then one of his fingers dipped into her entrance. "You are slick." He growled as his finger thrust into her, rubbing over her g-spot. "But are you slick enough?"

"The water will help." She panted. She had no idea if the water would indeed help, but she just wanted him to thrust his cock deep inside her. Her mind felt crazed with her desire. "Please." Stars!

Water sloshed violently around them as her hips ground against his hand. She needed release.

His fingers slipped from her, and before she could whine and complain about the loss, the head of his cock pressed against her entrance. She'd been right.

As the head of his cock slipped into her, he stretched her wide, and she knew he would be the best fit she ever had.

Akkon's hands grasped her hips, and he plunged into her. Straight to the hilt. Her breath caught in her chest as her body adjusted to his width. He didn't leave her any time to grow used to his length. Pumping his hips, he thrust in and out of her in long slow strokes.

Valeria's head lolled to the side as she let him fuck her. She didn't want to do anything other than let her eyes fall closed and let him build the climax within her. Her hands ran over his strong shoulders as he rammed into her. Sometimes a good fucking was the best kind of sex.

When Akkon withdrew from her core, she nearly shrieked at him to enter her again. Blinking, she asked, "What are you doing?"

"Wait and see." Was all she got. Akkon floated them over to the shallow side of the bathing pool, and then he swept her into his arms and placed her on the ground on her hands and knees. When she glanced over her shoulder, she found him kneeling on the first step of the bathing pool, his legs still semi in the water as he positioned his cock back at her entrance. Slamming forward, he groaned, and she moaned.

Thank the stars. Valeria had been worried for a second he might be ending their moment together.

One wandering hand found her clit, and she bucked back against him as his length stroked every delicate part of her and his finger circled her clit. So much sensation. So much pleasure. All she wanted was to plummet off the edge of the cliff. She bit down on her cheek, but she couldn't hold it back. As her insides clenched down around his cock she screamed his name. It echoed off the tiled walls and floors of the room.

"Yes, Valeria, take me." Akkon roared behind her as his hot seed seared through her. His finger never stopped circling her clit until they both returned to reality. Then his hand left her clit and gently massaged one orb of her ass.

Crawling forward, she pulled away from his cock and then flipped over onto her back to stare back at him. "I've never done it in a pool before."

"Nor have I." He winked. "I think it may be my favorite spot now. There are so many…" he motioned to the pool wall and then the ledge of the floor and stairs, "places where one could enjoy themselves."

"I want to lounge over there," Valeria pointed to a small area with pillows and blankets spread out, "with you, naked, enjoying this moment, but I also don't think we should be late to the council meeting."

"I'd prefer to skip it and explore your body some more." Akkon's hands whipped out and snatched her ankles, drawing her to him over the slick floor.

"Pfft, we can't skip it, Akkon. You need to show the councilors you are serious about taking back your position, which means you need to start now. Then you need to never miss a single meeting. Make your voice heard." She cocked her head to one side, her wet hair following the movement. "Do you not want to lead your people?"

"I do." He admitted. "I do." He leaned in closer to her. "Give me a kiss, and then we will head over to the council chamber."

Valeria leaned forward. His lips captured hers, and she melted. One of his hands groped her breast, and she laughed as she darted away to her feet. "Nope. You said one kiss, and we would go. No hanky panky for you until after we get back from the meeting."

Chapter 8

"The council meeting has been postponed until later." The Sri'thaen woman looked nervously from the screen in front of her to Akkon. "One of the councilors had a family emergency."

Valeria glanced over at him. "Can we at least go into the chamber? To see it?"

"Of course." Akkon placed a hand at the small of her back and led her forward past the woman sitting at the desk. "It will be empty, of course, but it will give you an idea of what it would look like full of people."

"I do have a good imagination."

They walked up to two large doors. Akkon placed a hand on each door and pushed them wide. Stepping inside, she found the room before her a decent size. Maybe it was a bit smaller than she would have expected. They stood up on a balcony of sorts. Beside her, there were several empty chairs. The rows rose progressively higher so each row could see over the head of the other. Below was a large empty area where someone would come to stand in front of the councilors.

"Where would you sit?" Valeria asked as she turned to look at Akkon.

"I would sit there." He rose a hand and pointed a finger up to the highest row where one chair sat alone. It was more intricate than the others. Each was carved from a white wood.

"It's beautiful." Valeria walked up the stairs until she stood before it. "Have you ever sat in it before?"

"No, I have not. But I am sure Zohx has kept it warm for me." His nostrils flared ever so slightly as he ground his teeth.

Valeria rolled her eyes. "You're making me think Zohx never wanted you to take control of your position. He saw a young boy he could manipulate, and he did."

"I think you make him out as more of an enemy than he really is."

Valeria turned with an arched eyebrow. "You are defending him?"

"Not defending him." Akkon shook his head sharply. "I simply think you're making him out worse than he is. If I show an interest in the people and show him how serious I am, I think he would welcome me with open arms."

Valeria snorted before covering her mouth with her hands. "I'm sorry. I don't want to appear rude, but I simply can't see him welcoming anyone with open arms. Is he even married?"

"No."

"Any prospects?"

"Why so curious about his personal life?"

Valeria's eyes danced over Akkon's face. He wasn't jealous. His jaw was loose, and his eyes studied her in return. "Just need to learn more about him. I feel as though he will always be there, lurking over your shoulder."

"I don't think any women are interested in Zohx."

"Oh?"

"If you're looking for gossip, you're looking in the wrong direction." Akkon held up his hands. "I was never one for listening to much gossip. Your fellow concubines might know more than myself."

"So," Valeria steered the conversation back to the chair. "If you've never sat in the chair before, do you want to now?"

Akkon's blue eyes shifted to the chair, and he nodded his head with a curt jerk. She stood back and watched as he walked up the stairs and then turned his back to the chair. Reaching behind him, he placed his hands on the armrests, and then seeming to take a moment, he sat.

Valeria strode up the stairs until she stood beside him. "How does it feel?"

"Powerful." He didn't even miss a beat in answering her.

"You could see yourself up here in the future?"

"I could." He confirmed. Then he turned his blue eyes to her. "I never would have thought to come here without you."

Valeria shrugged one shoulder. "I'm sure at some point you would have come here. How can a king ignore a throne? It's in your blood to want to sit here and rule."

Akkon snorted. "We have no thrones here."

"It's thrown like." Valeria reached out a hand and caressed the carved wood. "Someone spent time carving this."

"They did a marvelous job." Akkon agreed as his eyes shifted to the chair he sat on. "It's the same chair used by five generations of kings."

"Did your family always rule?" When he cocked his head to the side, she explained. "In the past, Earth had many kings in different countries. Back in the medieval times, thrones switched hands as family members fought for it."

"Ah." Akkon nodded his head. "My family has ruled for around eight centuries. Before that, it was another family. In the past, we had wars over the ruling of our planet, but since my family took over, it's been peaceful."

"Did Zohx's family rule before yours?"

Akkon chuckled as he leaned back in the chair. "You're looking for trouble where there is none. Zohx's family only came into power when mine did. He would have no entitlement to the throne, even if he wished otherwise." His hands zipped out, and he captured her around the waist, drawing her down upon his lap. "I need you," Akkon whispered hotly in her ear.

"The seat of power turning you on?" Valeria joked as a thrill raced up and down her spine.

He rocked his hips under her butt, and she sucked in a breath as his erection pressed into her. One of his hands slid under the waistband of her running pants. They hadn't changed after leaving the bathing pool. When he encountered no underwear, he growled approvingly into her ear. Shivers of excitement pulsed through her when his fingertip found her hot bud.

With his other hand, Akkon pulled the neckline of her shirt down, popping a breast over the line of fabric. His fingers rubbed both her clit and her nipple. Head falling back, Valeria let the pleasure ripple over her.

Desire ripped through Akkon as he watched Valeria's head fall back and her plump lips fall open. His gaze slipped from her face to her breast. The pink nipple stood out against her naturally tanned skin. When he'd first spotted her, he'd thought she'd been kissed by the sun. But now, after seeing her undress, he knew it had nothing to do with the sun. Humans intrigued him with their many skin colors. It was almost an entirely human trait. Most aliens had small differences between their own species.

Her nipple hardened under his touch, and pride soared through him. She enjoyed what he did to her, and he enjoyed what she did to him. Wetness grew between her legs as he flicked her clit. Her breaths became more labored, and her hips bucked.

Akkon's cock jumped. It felt near to bursting, completely ready to bury itself in her welcoming warmth, but he held back. As tempting as it, was he wanted to watch her shatter around his hand.

It only took a few minutes before she shattered in his arms. Quaking, she moaned loudly, filling the room with her pleasure. When her quaking subsided, Akkon removed his hand from her pants.

"Stand up." He commanded her.

With hazy eyes, Valeria stood up on shaky legs and faced him. Satisfaction hit him hard as he looked her up and down. She looked half-ravished when he'd barely touched her.

"Take off your pants."

Valeria didn't hesitate. She immediately bent

and disrobed, leaving just her shirt. He loved that she didn't question him. Simply obeyed. At least when it came to sex.

"Now, unbutton my pants," Akkon commanded. He wanted to command her to her knees and watch her crawl over to him, but they had plenty of time to play out every single naughty fantasy flying through his head.

With a confident smile, Valeria stepped up to him. Straddling his hips, her fingers quickly undid the belt at his waist. Then she unzipped his pants, and a gasp escaped her when his cock sprang free.

Her pink tongue darted out to wet her lips, and his cock pulsed in excitement.

Akkon hooked an arm around her waist, drawing her wet core right next to his cock, but it needed to wait. First, he intended to suck on that nipple that begged for more attention. It was like a stiff little beacon, drawing his focus.

A gasp escaped her as his mouth closed around the exposed nub. Sucking on it, he slowly drew loud moans from her mouth. A smile creased his lips as her pleasure flooded the room. She was exquisite. Her body burned hot for him and his touch, and it pleased him.

His hand wandered down to her thighs. He slipped a finger through her wet folds. Valeria was ready for him.

Akkon's cock jumped in excitement. Releasing her nipple with a smacking pop, he grabbed her hips and lifted her up.

Valeria gasped as her hands landed on his shoulders.

Anticipation surged through Valeria as Akkon held her braced above his cock. Then he surged her down, and she threw her head back as he fit her to the hilt.

"Akkon… yes.." She moaned as his cock stretched her wide. A thrill pierced her, knowing they were about to have sex in a more public area. Anyone could wander in and spot them. The woman outside could wonder about all the noise and pop her head in. It felt wicked.

Rotating her hips back and forth, she reveled in the feel of his cock deep inside her. His cock fit her so perfectly, hitting all the right parts.

"Move inside me, Akkon."

Akkon chuckled. "I think you forget who the king is."

She shook her head like a wild woman. "No, I don't command, I beg. Please."

Akkon's grip tightened on her waist, drawing her up his cock until just the wide tip stayed inside her pussy. Then he plunged her down. All her nerves seemed to light on fire as her cheeks burned with her desire. Each stroke of his cock sent her teetering on the edge.

"Soooo, close." She moaned. "Faster, Akkon, faster.

"I didn't hear a please."

The man infuriated her. Digging her fingernails into his shoulders, she managed to utter. "Please."

Immediately, his thrusts increased, sending her breasts bouncing, causing another sensation of pleasure to shoot through her. Her body couldn't handle much more before it broke.

Valeria cried his name mindlessly as her body neared its orgasm. Akkon groaned under her, whispering harsh encouragements.

Then her body tightened. Her pussy clenched, and she shattered.

Stars! Akkon groaned when her wet heat squeezed his cock, demanding his release. As much as he wanted to stop thrusting and shudder into her, he kept her bouncing a top him. Her tanned breasts danced wildly in front of him.

Akkon plowed as deep as his cock could reach. All the while, her pussy clenched around him, her moans growing in loudness as she sought her climax.

"Akkon. Akkon." She panted.

He watched her face until he saw it. Her mouth popped wide, and her body slumped as her hips jerked. Then and only then, he let his control slip.

Grunting his release, his hands tightened around her waist, continuing to thrust into her. His seed shot forth, covering the walls of her pussy. Even when he finished and stopped thrusting, her inner walls clenched around him, drawing his seed deeper into her.

A fleeting thought flowed through him that he could get her pregnant. Normally, he took precautions with women, but for some reason, it didn't trouble him. It might actually thrill him a little. He'd never entertained the idea of children, but maybe just maybe, he would now.

It was more difficult than Valeria wanted to admit to head back to the concubine room. But it had been a productive day. She still held out hope she didn't need to kill anyone to cause a bit of disruption in the Sri'thaen government. She hoped by Akkon claiming his rightful position, she could throw a plasma grenade right into the middle of it all. She simply needed to see where this went. Her mission wasn't supposed to be a fast fix. She needed to work slowly. Cause as much damage or disruption as she could.

When she entered the room, she found the other concubines seated in the lowered sitting area.

"How was your day?" Sar asked when she noticed Valeria in the doorway.

All the other women turned to stare up at her.

"We managed to find ourselves some fun." Valeria smiled as she took the couple of steps down into the sitting area. Plopping down on a cushion, she sighed. "We went for a run, then a bath, and then he showed me the council chamber."

Selde huffed and crossed her arms in front of her chest. The gold dress she wore went nicely with the purple hue of her skin. Even though the two of them didn't get along, Valeria couldn't deny the other woman's beauty. "It won't last. He will grow tired of you just like he did with us."

"Speak for yourself." Sar rolled her silver eyes. "He never showed any interest in me. Other than saving most of us, he hasn't even spared us a second look." Sar turned back to Valeria. "Did you have dinner?"

"Actually, no. We got…" Valeria felt her cheeks flush, and for the first time in her life, it wasn't forced. "We got distracted." A lot. After their romp in the meeting chamber, it seemed to be Akkon's mission to take her in every other spot he could think of inside the palace.

Sar and Fanka clapped their hands together.

Selde huffed. Rising quickly, she stormed out of the lowered sitting area with her cronies hot on her heels.

"Now that they're gone," Valeria scooted closer to the other three. "I need some information."

"Oh?" Alvae asked as she passed a plate to Sar, who passed the plate over to Valeria.

"I think I need to know more about this Zohx character. Who is he exactly?" Valeria asked as she took a piece of what appeared to be cheese off her plate. The greenish hue of it was a bit unnerving, but she doubted Akkon would serve poisonous food to his concubines. He seemed thoughtful when it came to the women.

"Zohx is definitely a man to be careful of around here." Sar looked to the other women. "I can't say I've had much interaction with him before, but there's something about him." She shivered. "I have no doubt he would kill if ever given the reason."

Valeria selected another slice of the green cheese. It was good. She had no idea what animal they milked to make it, but the light fruity and tangy taste was delectable.

"I've crossed his path a couple of times as well, and he definitely sends a shiver up my spine." Alvae agreed. "Not that he's ever done anything." She held up a hand. "It was simply a feeling in his presence."

"Is he from a powerful family?"

"Second to the king's probably." Sar squinted as she thought. "Then there is Rakshasas. His family is also just as old as the others."

"I believe I may have heard of Rakshasas's name before," Valeria commented.

"A ruthless general that one." Fanka nodded her head. "But very handsome. I've seen him a couple of times, and I wouldn't mind welcoming a man like that into my bed."

Sar gasped. "Don't let Adira hear you say that, or you will disappear and never be heard from again."

Valeria cocked her head to the side. "Is that his wife?"

"It is." Sar's eyes narrowed on Valeria, and for a brief second Valeria tensed. "I suppose you might not know. Adira is human."

Valeria raised a hand to her mouth as she choked on her cheese. "Excuse me. What?"

"Adira is Rakshasas's wife, and she is not a woman to mess with."

Valeria was surprised to hear a Sri'thaen and a general had married a human. With how the Sri'thaen's felt about humans, she simply figured it wouldn't happen. Then again, she was with the Sri'thaen king.

"How long have they been together?"

"Not too long. Definitely less than half a year, and from what I've seen, they are madly in love with each other. If you see one, the other won't be far away. No babies yet, though, but I'm sure there is no lack of trying."

"Well, give it time. I don't know about Sri'thaen reproductive times, but humans can take some time." Valeria snagged another slice of the cheese. "So not much else to pass along about Zohx?"

"He keeps to himself." Sar shrugged as she leaned back, draping her body elegantly across the soft pillows.

Compared to Valeria, the other concubines were supermodels. Then again, maybe she was being unfair to herself. The king didn't seem to mind her looks, which should speak volumes. He hadn't touched any of these women, yet he appeared to like her. Although she supposed his attentions could wane.

"If there's no more to pass along, then I am heading for bed with my dinner. It sounds like Akkon might invite me along when he attends a councilor meeting tomorrow, and I want to make sure I'm energized and ready to go." Valeria stood with a plate of food.

"Sleep well." The women called out as she left their area and headed for her room.

"Valeria."

Stopping, Valeria glanced over her shoulder to see Selde standing nearby. "Yes?"

"I wanted to apologize for my reaction to your introduction."

Valeria prevented her mouth from dropping open. An apology from Selde was the last thing she ever expected. "Um, thanks. Your apology is accepted." Turning, she brought her plate to her room. After she ate some dinner and let the shock of Selde's apology ease, she prepped her hair for tomorrow. She wanted to look her best.

"What is," Sar pointed to Valeria's head the next morning, "going on up there?" She moved her hand in a circle as she continued pointing.

"What do you mean?" Valeria asked as she brought the outfit she'd chosen over to her vanity. When she sat down in front of the mirror, she gasped. "What the hell is wrong with my hair?" She raised her hands to the frizzy mass around her head. Every single strand seemed to be tangled and standing on end like someone had zapped her with a plasma stick.

"I'm guessing you weren't trying some new hairdo then?"

"New? This is ugly!" Valeria shook her head. Grabbing a comb, she worked on her hair, only to find the rat's nests in her hair too hard to get through. "If Akkon actually brings me to the council meeting, I can't look like this! I'll embarrass him." He might even wonder if she had done this on purpose. They didn't know each other well, and she didn't wish to break any trust between them. Otherwise, she might find herself discarded like the other concubines.

Her eyes darted around as she tried to figure out what happened. "Is there something in the atmosphere that screws with hair?"

Sar laughed. "If it affected your hair, then it would most likely affect us all." She pursed her lips as her eyes scanned over Valeria's table. "Maybe you used a wrong cream or hair product?"

"I used this." Valeria held up a small silver jar.

Sar took it from her, popped open the little lid, and then raised it to her nose. Immediately, she scrunched her nose. "I think a prank may have been played on you." She held the jar down. "Give it a sniff."

Valeria leaned in and sucked in a deep breath. Leaning back, she shrugged her shoulders. "I don't smell anything."

"Oh." Sar blinked. "Maybe humans can't smell *ginga*."

"*Ginga*?"

"It's an herb native to this planet. It's mainly used to flavor food. It tastes better than it smells."

Valeria lifted the jar to her nose and sniffed it again. She still couldn't smell anything. With a sigh, she tossed it into the pretty trash bin next to her table. "Well, can we do something about this?" She waved a hand at her hair.

"I'll need to collect some herbs and rub it into your hair, but it will require me to ask for a visit to the local market."

"Sounds like it will take a while then." Valeria grumped. Which meant she might not be able to go to the meeting with Akkon. There was a part of her that feared he wouldn't go if she didn't go with him.

"It will. Sorry."

"So, what do we do about it then?" At this point, she might be willing to shave her head and wear a wig. Assuming Sri'thaens made wigs.

"We can tie it down as much as possible."

"Would you mind helping me?" Valeria asked. She felt a bit deflated. She'd woken with such high hopes for the day. She was close to the king, and she was in a perfect position to cause chaos among the high-ranking officials of the Sri'thaen government. Zohx was about to get the wake up call of his life. Once she was done here, it wouldn't be him calling the shots.

"Of course!" Sar said as her silver eyes met Valeria's brown ones in the mirror. Reaching out, she grabbed supplies off the top of the table and started working on the mess of hair.

A light snicker had both of their heads snapping around. Selde stood with her cronies, watching them. Her purple arms were folded across her chest, and her violet lips turned up in a sneer.

Valeria's eyes narrowed on the other woman as realization dawned on her. She had been the butt of a prank, and she planned to repay Selde in kind. "We have a saying on my home planet. Be careful when playing with fire, Selde. You might get burned." She warned before turning back to the mirror.

Selde huffed, and she heard their footsteps fade as she and her group left.

"I like that one," Sar commented. "I will have to remember it."

"While you're at it, think of a way for us to get her back. If she wants a war, then a war she will get." Valeria promised. "It's time she was set back in her place." She wished she could do something more to Selde than a simple prank, but as annoying as the woman might be, she wasn't a huge danger. Otherwise, Valeria might look at getting rid of the woman more permanently.

Sar smiled at her in the mirror. "I knew we would be fast friends. Now I know why." Sighing, Sar shook her head. "I think the only solution right now is to throw your hair into a bun and hope for the best."

"I guess that will have to do." As long as she was presentable, she was okay with whatever. As long as they got to the councilor meeting. That's all that mattered to her.

"Excuse me." A masculine voice called out.

Shifting in her seat, Valeria glanced over to see a Sri'thaen guard standing beside the door to the concubines' rooms. His back was ram rod straight, and she wondered if it was his tight black clothing or the fact he was a guard. Either way, it didn't look comfortable.

"I am here for Valeria. The king has asked for her."

"I am here." Valeria raised a hand. "Just give me a second."

"The king waits for no one." The guard

growled.

Valeria rolled her eyes and turned back to the mirror. “Quick, Sar. You heard the man. The king waits for no one.”

Laughing under her breath, Sar quickly tied up Valeria’s hair at the back of her neck. Once Sar finished, Valeria gave it a cursory look before darting up from her seat and dashing for the door.

“Have fun!” Sar called out.

Valeria waved and caught sight of Selde glaring at her from the other side of the room. She could expect more tricks coming from that woman. And it might be worse than hair cream. That woman was her greatest enemy, would always be sniffing around, searching for a way to get rid of Valeria in hopes of being the king’s favorite once more.

Perhaps she could figure out a way to get rid of Selde. As she followed the guard, she decided she would try. If the king wasn’t interested in any of them, then he shouldn’t have any issue with getting rid of some of his concubines. She just needed to bring it up delicately. Men in power preferred to think ideas came from them, not those around them, and they definitely didn’t enjoy receiving orders.

For the first time in her job, Valeria experienced a flutter in her stomach. She wasn’t used to experiencing nerves. Every mission she walked in with her head held high and determination burning in her heart. Yet, she felt the prickle of anxiety run over her spine and scalp. For some reason, she wanted Akkon to release his concubines with little to no effort.

Valeria pursed her lips in frustration. She didn’t like this new her. Hardening her feelings, she shoved her worries down. She was here to assassinate, gather intel, and or cause whatever chaos she could. And that was exactly what she would do.

She didn't wish to examine these flittering feelings in her stomach. Examining feelings would only clutter her thoughts and hinder her mission. All she needed to worry about was Akkon claiming his throne and then whispering in his ear until she got things changed. It was as simple as that.

Chapter 9

Akkon rubbed a hand over his heart. The frantic pitter patter caused him to wonder what it meant. Never before had he felt nervous before meeting a woman. Then again, he had never met a woman quite like Valeria. For the first time in a long time, a woman held his attention. It wasn't just her beautiful tanned skin and brunette hair. No woman before her challenged him to be a better man.

Excitement pulsed through him as he thought about the turn his life would take as he took charge of his people and their welfare. There would be no more boring same routine after same routine. Instead, every day would bring a new challenge. He couldn't say he was ready. There would be a learning curve, he was sure, but with Valeria cheering him on, he knew he could do it.

"Your Majesty." A guard entered the room, his back stiff as he nodded to Akkon.

"Akkon!" Valeria bounced around the guard, a smile on her lips.

The guard's eyes and mouth popped open. When he made a movement to reach for Valeria, to stop her, Akkon strode forward, taking her arm and guiding her away from the guard.

"It is good to see you again." His eyes traveled over her and stopped on her hair. "You may go." He said to the guard without looking up. The loud footsteps of the guard let him know his order was being fulfilled. "Isn't your hair normally straight?" He asked as he raised a finger to a stray curl.

"Oh." A dark flush hinted behind her brown skin. "I fear I used a wrong product on my hair last night, and it resulted in some… disturbing effects."

He chuckled. "I hope none of the women have been bothering you."

Valeria's eyes narrowed up at him. Those dark brown eyes almost looked black, and they drew him in. "Have you heard something?"

"Should I have heard something?"

"Don't worry about me, Akkon." She sent him a smile. "I can handle myself if I ever run into any problems."

"But I do hope you will let me know if anyone is ever hurtful." A frown turned his lips down. "I won't tolerate anyone being hurtful to each other."

"No one has been hurtful."

Akkon inclined his head when he heard the truth in her words. "Then I will let the subject drop. Shall I escort you to the council chamber?"

"Please." Valeria took his arm when he held it out to her, and his chest puffed out. "I must admit, I am excited to see my first Sri'thaen council meeting. I have to imagine no human has seen one."

Akkon chuckled. "You would not be the first."

"Oh, yes, that's right. You said something about a human."

When he glanced over at her, he found her watching him with those intelligent brown eyes. "I would imagine the concubines have talked about it with you as well."

"I might have heard something about a human woman being married to a Sri'thaen general, but hearing it from your mouth would let me know it's true."

"It's true." Akkon looked forward as he led them through the halls of the palace. "One of our best general's found a human spy, and before anyone knew it, he was smitten." Their love was a strange one. He knew Rakshasas decently well, but he'd only met Adira a couple of times. She was an angry human. He could say that about her. Whatever Earth government had done to her must have been horrible. He couldn't claim to have the full story.

"How did they meet?"

"She was sent as a spy. I can't say I know much more than that. They tend to keep to themselves."

"You're king. Shouldn't you know more about your general's life?"

Akkon's gaze slid to Valeria. She stared straight ahead as they walked, allowing him a moment to take her in. She felt unafraid to question him, a king, about how he did things. It was fortunate she found him as king. Kings didn't normally enjoy being questioned or challenged. From the few memories he had of his father, he knew from experience kings didn't enjoy incessant questions. He remembered the sting on his father's hand smacking the back of his head several times.

"When you meet them, you will understand why no one, not even I, butt into their lives." Adira and Rak scared him. They scared anyone who met them. The two loved each other as much as they loved torturing and killing people.

Valeria raised her eyebrows as she faced him. "You're scared of them?"

"They make everyone they meet shit their pants."

Valeria snorted before covering her mouth with a hand. "I can't wait to meet them. Tell me you'll make sure it happens."

He cringed. If he could prevent it, he would make sure they never met. With Valeria's uncensored mouth, he feared her angering Adira and getting her head blasted off. His arm tightened around her arm until she growled at him.

"Akkon!" She barked under her breath when he didn't hear her.

Releasing his grip on her arm, he muttered an apology.

He stopped them short of the council chamber door. Turning to Valeria, he met her eyes and held them. "Do try to keep a hold of your tongue." When she blustered, he held a finger to her mouth. "I enjoy your opinions and your lack of fear voicing them, but not all the councilors will find it so endearing. Let's try to earn their favor." Especially since he wanted to keep her around.

Valeria nodded. "Believe me or not, but I can keep my mouth shut when the need arises."

Akkon's eyebrows nearly jumped off his forehead before he could stop himself.

"What?" Valeria planted her hands on her hips. "I can!"

"Then prove it." He challenged her.

Steel flashed in those beautiful eyes, and he

knew she would to prove him wrong. Good. He didn't need her insulting everyone in the room. There was only so much mouthy human they could take, and they already barely tolerated Adira.

"Now, let us attend the meeting before it finishes with us still standing here in the hallway."

"Lead the way, and I will be sure to follow like the dutiful and subservient concubine," Valeria promised.

Akkon snorted. "We will see." If she managed to pull it off, he would eat his shoe.

Raising his hands, he rested them on the dark wood of the council chamber door. This would be the first meeting he'd attended in years. There was a tremor of fright in his stomach. He wouldn't admit it to anyone, but he felt scared he would enter the chamber and fall flat on his face.

Pushing forward, the door creaked open lightly, and he entered the chamber. His eyes skimmed over the gathered councilors and his eyes landed at the top most seat. It wasn't empty. Zohx sat comfortably in the king's chair.

His jaw tightened as he ground his teeth together. It took a human woman to point out how far he'd let the councilors walk all over him and his position. He had eyes. He should have seen it long before now.

"Zohx." Akkon greeted as he walked up the steps. "I thank you for keeping my seat warm, but as you can see, I am here and ready to take it."

He watched Zohx's jaw tense, but the man did rise. If slowly. But he did vacate the seat. With a stiff bow, Zohx inclined his head to Akkon. "I am glad to see you've taken a sudden interest. Please let me know if there is anything I can explain."

Barely preventing the growl clawing its way up his throat, Akkon plastered a fake smile on his face. "I thank you." Then he sat down in the chair.

Zohx turned to leave and then froze. His eyes zeroed in on a spot behind Akkon.

Turning slightly in his seat, Akkon found Valeria standing slightly behind his seat. "This is Valeria."

"A concubine." Zohx hissed. "A human concubine. In the meeting chamber?"

Akkon bristled. He didn't like the way Zohx said human or concubine. "She is to be given the same respect as a *Mora*."

Zohx blinked at Akkon. "Like a *Mora*?"

"She has earned my trust and respect."

"But she is not your *Mora*?"

"No," Akkon shook his head, "she is not."

Zohx's cold eyes narrowed on Valeria. "Whatever you wish, Your Majesty." He bowed once more before finding a seat on one of the lower levels.

As the councilors talked amongst each other, Valeria crouched beside his chair and asked, "I don't think he likes me any more than the other time he met me. Seems to be a hard to figure out individual."

"You've heard of him?"

"The other concubines talked about him. Nothing too fond either."

Akkon wasn't surprised to hear it. Zohx probably caused his own mother to shiver in fear. Could anyone predict Zohx or read him? The man was a closed book, and he struck before anyone saw what was coming.

"Why was he in your seat?"

Clutching the armrests of the chair, Akkon muttered under his breath. "It seems you came into my life at the right moment."

"Oh?"

"I never had any reason to take control of my councilors. I'd grown used to them overseeing things and thought I could trust them. It seems as though some, like Zohx, wanted nothing more than to play king." And it burned inside him. How could he have let it get this far? These were his people. Never again. The councilors would have no choice but to grow used to him being around from now on because he intended to have his nose in any business that affected the Sri'thaen people.

Pride bubbled up inside Valeria's chest as she crouched beside Akkon's seat and watched him handle the minor issues being brought up. After the councilors stopped gabbing about Akkon being present, the Sri'thaen public filtered through the room. It seemed the problems went through a court system, and then if unresolved or if one of the parties wanted it to go higher, then they came here looking for the councilors and the king to settle the matter. Problems ranged from a stolen shuttle to more serious offenses like trying to reduce the number of years in jail. Then there were the cases where people wanted special licenses to build on government land.

"We can help–"

She tuned out Zohx as he spoke. "Are you going to let him make the final decision on everything brought to the council's attention? I thought we were here to make a point. For them to take you seriously as you stepped into the position of king." She whispered to Akkon, making sure the only one who heard her was him.

"Zohx." Akkon rose from his seat.

Zohx turned, his mouth snapping shut. She saw his jaw flex. The man didn't do well getting knocked down a peg. Satisfaction swelled inside her chest. She didn't honestly know Zohx, but for some reason, watching his discomfort satisfied her.

"We will consider your idea for a complex on the west side of the capital city, but," Akkon glanced down at the pad in front of him, "you come dangerously close to our sacred forest. The animals and plant life there are not to be disturbed. If heavy equipment shakes the ground, they will no doubt become distraught." When the man below them began to open his mouth, Akkon raised a hand. "Come back when your building plan includes a way to prevent from bothering the animals there."

"But we… we've put money into this project, and we have men ready to begin the building." The man stuttered as his eyes darted between Akkon and Zohx, seeming uncertain which man to look at.

"I understand. Unfortunately, these laws have been in place for years, and they were put in place for a reason. We must preserve nature for those to come after us." Akkon sat back down. "We will see you when you have a plan that includes consideration for the animals in the nearby forest." He waved a hand, and a guard stepped forward, ushering the man out of the room.

Zohx cast a glare up at them, which Akkon missed, but Valeria caught. She smirked, and when he caught sight of it, his eyes narrowed on her.

She'd faced worse foes than Zohx. Normally, when she was on a mission, she kept to herself and tried not to draw too much attention to herself. But here? Here she had a king on her side, at least for now. It bestowed greater confidence in her when it came to facing down Zohx and letting him know exactly who his new enemy was.

"Sit, Zohx." Akkon demanded when he saw the councilor still stood. "We have another of our people waiting to bring us their important issue, and you are delaying matters."

With one last glare sent her way, Zohx took his seat stiffly.

A smile spread across her face. She felt certain Zohx would present her with a fun challenge. More of a challenge than Selde and her silly childish pranks.

Listening to the people's issues took the rest of the day. As the councilors filed out of the room, Akkon rose and placed a hand to Valeria's back, ushering her out. He guided her through the palace. When they reached the bathing chamber, the area between her legs heated, knowing exactly what would happen while they were here.

The door closed behind them and in the blink of an eye, Akkon pressed her up against the cool, tiled wall.

"I know it's bad, but I had nothing on my

mind except you all day. I wondered if we would ever find a moment to break away." Akkon murmured huskily.

Valeria smiled at his words. It flattered her. No matter how much she tried to remember this was a job, she kept forgetting. That was the problem with sex. It might start as a tool, but it could grow out of control in the blink of an eye. Already she felt something like affection growing for Akkon. The Sri'thaen king wasn't like she'd expected. He may not have been the best king to start with, but it wasn't like anyone had taught him better. Now, though, he was stepping up and taking his position back.

Akkon thrust his hips against her, allowing her to feel his throbbing erection through his pants.

Gasping, Valeria reached out, tugging the hem of his shirt up and over his head. Her hands skimmed over his toned pecs as he placed hot kisses to her neck.

"You're like an addiction," Akkon muttered in between kisses.

"I'd say sorry, but it'd be a lie."

Akkon chuckled. Pulling away with a groan, his eyes raked over her. "Undress." Then he stripped his shoes and pants.

Valeria followed suit, quickly stripping her clothes off.

Once they were both nude, Akkon led her over to the edge of the bathing water. She would call it a pool if she didn't know better.

Akkon walked backward into the water, and she took a moment to admire him. His body wasn't overly muscled. He possessed a six pack, but his arms and chest were just perfect. He didn't scare her with his muscles. She had no doubt he could easily take her out, but he wasn't overly muscled like a body builder. He reminded her more of a lean, toned cat than a lumbering bear.

"Are you coming?"

Akkon's voice jolted her from her musings. "Yes." She murmured huskily as she stepped into the warm water.

Akkon's blue eyes watched her every move like a predator. He knew what he wanted, and it was her. Her heart fluttered in her chest. Once waist deep in the water, she walked over to him.

"Our first meeting always plays in my head. Teases me until my cock is so stiff I can barely tolerate it." He said as he brought her into his arms.

"It was thrilling." Valeria agreed, loving how his hands wandered over her back and buttocks, massaging the flesh. With his hands resting against her butt, he pressed her into him, flattening her breasts against his chest. Valeria sucked in a breath. It amazed her how simple touches could set her blood on fire.

"Should we wash each other?" Akkon asked, his voice gone husky and low.

All Valeria could do was nod her head, her voice seeming stuck in her throat.

Breaking away from her, Akkon walked over to the side of the bathing pool. He held his hands up to a small device at the edge of the pool, and it squirted out a purple liquid. Then he rubbed his hands together as he walked over to her. "Let me."

His large hands landed on her shoulders, and he rubbed the soap over her skin. His fingers worked her flesh until her shoulders slumped in relaxation. Slowly, he worked his way down her chest until he reached her breasts. His hands easily encompassed her generous breasts, the palms rubbing against her sensitive nipples.

Valeria's eyes sank closed as he massaged her breasts. He plucked at her nipples, and she gasped. Her legs wobbled, and she felt like they might give way under her. Just as quickly as his hands landed on her breasts, they glided down to her sides until they dipped under the water.

"Part your legs." He commanded.

Valeria spread her legs, and his hand dipped into the junction. She figured most all of the soap was gone, and much wasn't getting washed anymore. Not that she minded.

Akkon's exploring fingers found the lips of her pussy. Pressing a couple of them forward, he spread them. Then his fingers found her clit, and with an expert touch, he rubbed the pad of one finger over it.

Valeria bit the inside of her cheek as her knees shook and sensation rolled through her. Her pussy throbbed, knowing exactly what was to come.

Reaching out a hand, Valeria balanced herself with the help of his shoulder. She reached out her other hand under the water until her fingers bumped into his rigid cock. Wrapping her hand around it, she stroked it up and down in slow, long strokes.

Akkon trembled as his fingers continued rubbing her nub.

"Only fair if we both get to come at the same time," Valeria whispered hotly.

He growled in agreement, and when she met his blue eyes, they'd gone dark and hazy with his desire.

Valeria pumped his cock, stroking the length and showing the tip some love with light squeezes of her fist.

Akkon's fingers slipped down through her folds until he reached the entrance of her pussy. Two of his fingers slipped into her. He found her g-spot and applied pressure as he stroked his fingers in and out of her.

"Kiss me." Valeria tilted her head up, and his mouth covered hers without hesitation. His strong lips melded against hers, and the tip of his tongue glided against the seam of her lips until she parted for him. Taking advantage, his tongue slid into her mouth, dancing with hers before pulling back.

A moan escaped Valeria as his fingers stroked deep inside her. As her knees trembled, she was thankful for the support of the water around her. The thrusts of his fingers increased with the rhythm of her hand on his cock.

"Oh, Akkon, I'm so close."

"Let me hear you," Akkon commanded as his head bent further, capturing a nipple in his mouth.

"Oh, yeah!" Valeria's head fell back as she moaned her words up to the ceiling.

Akkon groaned, "Fuck."

Then they both shuttered together. Her hand jolted in short thrusts over his cock as he shot his seed into the water.

About a week later, Valeria stretched out on the lowered sitting area and marveled at her luck. This mission was less a mission and more like a vacation. She had a sexy king courting her… well, maybe courting was the wrong word. She had a king interested in her, and she lived in the lap of luxury with the other concubines. Maybe she should switch careers. All she had to find was a sexy, well off man, and she'd have it made for the rest of her life as a concubine.

"I see you're having no trouble finding a place for yourself," Sar commented from where she lounged.

"In what way?"

"The king seems to value your opinion. Why else would he continue to bring you to all those councilor meetings?"

"Jealous?" Valeria felt disappointment soar through her. She hoped out of everyone, Sar wouldn't begrudge her a place by the king.

"Not at all!" Sar laughed. "I would be so bored sitting in one of those meetings, let alone several. I'm happy one of us finally pleases him. I always wondered why he never used any of us. Perhaps he simply hadn't found the woman with the right interests." Sar winked over at her. "Maybe you could become queen."

Valeria snorted and waved away the absurd idea. She had no ambitions to become queen of an alien race. She doubted the Sri'thaen people wished to see a human sitting on the throne. Then again, she hadn't met many Sri'thaens outside of the palace. Maybe she should reserve her assumptions until she knew the people better. "I think I tickle his fancy… for now."

"For now? I don't think you see the way he–"

A shriek cut off the last part of Sar's sentence. "Look at my face! Look at my face!"

Sar and Valeria shared a knowing glance.

"What happened?" Aphe asked as she stopped rubbing cream into her powder blue skin.

"Someone messed with my face cream, and now look at my face!" Selde screeched again.

Valeria snickered, and Sar shushed her. "Don't give us away."

"Where is that human? I know it was her." Selde vented.

Valeria shrugged at Sar.

Sar shook her head and whispered, "I came up with the idea, but we both implemented it. Why do you get all the credit?"

"Because she hates me more than you, so it's easy and more fun for her to blame me." Valeria snorted.

A raging Selde stormed over to where they sat, and when Valeria's eyes landed on her, her eyes bulged. What the stars had Sar put in the cream jar? Large purple bumps covered Selde's face. They ran all the way from her temple to her throat.

"What have you done?" Selde blustered from above her.

"I didn't do anything." Valeria shrugged a shoulder. If the other woman attacked, she wasn't scared. She knew how to fight, and she doubted Selde did. Selde used words and other people around her to defeat enemies. She would never want to break a nail or get a hair out of place.

"Do you see this?" Selde pointed to her face. "Do you see what you've done to me? What if the king asks to see me?"

Sar snorted and announced loudly, "He hasn't asked for you since I arrived in this harem."

Selde blustered as she tried to figure out her next words.

"Instead of standing here blaming me, maybe you should take care of those bumps," Valeria suggested. "I think you might be having an allergic reaction. Would hate for it to clog your throat."

Selde raised a finger and pointed at her. "You'll rue this day, human. I'll make sure you never steal the king from me." Then she spun with a flutter of hair and dress.

Once she was gone, Valeria rolled her eyes with a sigh. "Why is she so obsessed with the king? Is she in love with him?" She could see how women would fall for him. He was nothing but nice and sexy.

"Selde? Love? I don't think she knows the definition of the word." Sar rose into a sitting position, tucking the flowing layers of her dress under her. "She has dreams of being queen or at least being the favorite concubine. She wants power."

Who didn't want power? Valeria could understand Selde's motivation. It was the same reason she loved her job. Whether her targets knew it or not, she held all the power. She could destroy them or raise them up. It all depended on her mission.

"A note for Valeria just arrived!" Fanka announced as she bounded over to their seats.

"Who is it from?" Sar asked loudly, and Valeria knew she did it just for Selde's sake.

"The king!" Fanka frowned. "Who else would it be from?"

Sar motioned to Valeria. "She's a pretty human. Maybe someone else took notice of her."

Fanka handed the note down to Valeria.

The paper felt silky smooth, and she marveled over the pretty letters of her name on the front. Flipping it over, she slid a finger between the envelope and the flap. Breaking the seal, she slid out the note and read over the words.

"What is it?" Sar asked.

"The king has invited me to a ball." Valeria felt some panic fill her chest. A ball sounded so formal and important.

Fanka sighed as she walked into their sitting area. "It sounds romantic."

Valeria rolled her eyes as she shoved the note back into the envelope. Sar held out her hand, and Valeria gave the note over.

"We have to get you a dress, and we don't have long." Sar looked up from the invitation. "It's only a few nights away."

"See? Something like this is planned months in advance. Him inviting me was just an afterthought."

"He only just met you." Sar tisked her tongue. "How was he to know he would want to take you to a ball?"

Maybe Sar was right, but Valeria didn't want to read too much into his motivation on inviting her. This was a mission. Even as she reminded herself of that, her heart skipped excitedly in her chest. She couldn't say she'd ever been to a ball, and there was a flicker of excitement in her.

Chapter 10

Waiting patiently wasn't one of Akkon's skills. It took Valeria about a day to respond to his invitation. All the time he worried she might reject him. Then when she did respond with a yes, she hadn't wanted him to see her outfit, even though he was the one who paid for it. Now he waited outside the concubine rooms. He was allowed inside, but he liked to give the women their own space where he, rarely if ever, intruded.

Pacing, his heart hammered in his throat. There was always the chance Valeria could change her mind. He sucked in a breath through his nose and let it out through his mouth. He wanted nothing more than to show her off to his people.

The doors creaked open, and he straightened to attention. Valeria emerged, and his breath caught in his chest as his eyes moved from the top of her head to the bottom of her dress. She wore a dark purple gown with swirling gold decorations across the bodice with swirls dipping onto the skirt of the dress. Her breasts were presented like a satin wrapped gift - lifted high into the air. As his eyes drifted back up, he found a purple and gold mask obscuring the top half of her face from his view. He did notice her hair had been done up to hide her rounded ears.

Good. His directions had been followed. He didn't need everyone swarming her immediately when they walked in. Sri'thaens had double-pointed ears, and anyone with eyes would notice hers were different. He knew it wouldn't take long for word to get out at the ball. People knew he had a human concubine, but they might not suspect he would be brazen enough to bring her with him. Not only was she a concubine, but a human. As his eyes skimmed over her, he knew he couldn't hide her. Knew he didn't want to hide her. He wasn't ashamed of Valeria. Whether or not she knew it, she'd become his rock in this short period of time. She was solid and always there for him as he grew into his position as king.

"How do you like it?" Valeria spun around in a circle, the skirt of the dress fanning out.

"Beautiful." Akkon wished more elegant words would come to his tongue, but nothing seemed adequate. "I have something for you." He held up the flat black box in his hands.

Valeria glided forward, took the box, and tipped the lid open. She gasped as her eyes went wide. "This is... stunning."

"It's for you."

"I," she shook her head, "I can't accept something like this. This must have cost..." She drifted off as she appeared to not know what number to assign it.

"I am a king. I haven't splurged much in my life. I think my people can excuse me this once when your lovely neck deserves nothing less." Akkon took the necklace out of the box. "Now turn."

Valeria didn't resist. Spinning around, she waited. Akkon slipped his arms over her head, placed the necklace against her throat, and clasped the necklace. Then he fluffed her hair out, hiding the back of the necklace.

"You can turn around now."

She did, and a giant smile adorned her lips as she raised a hand to the necklace. "Thank you, Akkon. No one has ever given me something this special."

His heart soared straight into the sky. He wouldn't lie. Pleasure filled him that he was the first to buy her something so special.

"Would you like to join the others in the ballroom?" He asked as he offered her an arm.

"Would I ever. I've never been to a ball, let alone an alien ball. Are there any traditions or rules I need to follow?" Valeria asked as her hand slipped over his arm, allowing him to guide them through the palace.

"I'm not sure if anything would be different than a human ball." Akkon thought back on the few he attended over the years. "We will be presented as we enter. There will be drinks, food, and dancing." He glanced over at her. "I assume you know not to wear red."

Valeria nodded. "Yes. Red can cause Sri'thaen men to lose their minds."

Akkon nodded as he shrugged a shoulder. "Yes and no. Some Sri'thaen men can resist the urge, but it is difficult. Most who can are already in a relationship with someone they love, but a single Sri'thaen? Good luck. Our doctors have experimented with medicine, but… no luck as of yet. It is illegal to wear red in public."

"Good to know. Would hate to be arrested." Her hand squeezed his arm as she sent him a wink.

Akkon chuckled. "It is fortunate you know the king. I'm sure I could figure a way out of prison for you."

Valeria smiled up at him, her eyes glittering with happiness as she gazed up at him from behind her mask. Leaning down, he caught her lips with his. She molded against him like it was the most natural thing in the world.

"I've been thinking." He prompted as he led her down the hall once they broke the kiss.

"Oh?"

"I hate seeing you leave my rooms at night. I think we should move your things into my chambers."

Valeria halted beside him, forcing him to stop walking since their arms were still joined. "Are you asking me to move in with you?"

Akkon took a second to mull over her words. In many ways, she already lived with him by staying in the palace, but yes, he wanted her closer. "I suppose the answer is yes."

"What will people think?"

"Does it matter?" He quickly responded, fearing she might draw back and say no. He would feel such a fool if she didn't return his feelings.

"Not to me."

Relief washed through him, causing his head to go dizzy. "I'm happy to hear you say that. I will have some guards move your things to my room while we are at the ball."

"Eager much?" She laughed.

"I want to wake with you in my arms," Akkon said as he drew her into his arms and pushed her up against a wall. Leaning in, he placed a kiss to her lips, and then to the juncture of her neck and shoulder. "I want to enjoy a warm breakfast in bed with you."

Valeria sent him another heart-stuttering smile. "I feel the same."

"Good." He growled in satisfaction. As he led them further down the hall, he willed his cock to go down. His robes weren't made of a thick material, and with a quick glance down, he made out the bulge.

"We're here." He whispered as he turned his attention to the open doors ahead of them. The sound of voices and music filtered out.

"I'm a bit nervous," Valeria whispered.

"You'll do fine," Akkon reassured her as they stepped through the door, and a man in a black outfit stepped forward.

"The king and…" the man's eyes moved over Valeria, "and guest." Then the man stepped back into his place by the door.

Akkon led her down a wide staircase to the main floor. The area swarmed with people as they danced, ate, and gossiped. Every woman wore their best dress and jewels while the men wore their fine robes.

"Your Majesty."

Akkon turned to find Zohx approaching. A small woman stood beside him, her arm draped through Zohx's. "Zohx. Managed to find a woman who isn't scared of you?"

Zohx's fake smile faltered on his face before recovering. "Indeed. She seems to find me irresistible. No matter how much I wish she would stay away, I find her by me all the time."

Akkon didn't miss it when the woman's eyes

turned to glare up at Zohx. Her hair was done down in the same fashion as Valeria's, and she also wore a mask that hid the top half of her face, only allowing her eyes, mouth, and chin to be visible. "Have I met you before?"

"I doubt it." The woman said as she inclined her head to Akkon.

"We must continue saying our hellos," Zohx said as he practically dragged the woman away.

"Enjoy the ball," Akkon said to the both of them before leading Valeria away. The moment Zohx heard he was welcoming the human concubine into his personal chambers, he knew Zohx would have an opinion.

"Would you care to dance?" Akkon leaned into Valeria's ear so he would be heard over the noise.

"I can't say I'm a good dancer, but I'm game."

Akkon chuckled. "Luckily for you, it's the man's job to lead, and if he's good enough, no one should ever know you're not a good dancer." He promised.

To Valeria's amazement, Akkon had been right. He soared her straight over the dance floor, and she felt as light as air as he guided her flawlessly into swirls and dips. Her dress's floor-length material hid any of her missteps, though she didn't suffer from many.

After a few songs, Akkon guided them over to the sidelines so they could catch their breaths. The room, although large, was pretty well packed full of people, and the heat was becoming stifling.

"Would you like to make your way to one of the balconies while I fetch us something to drink?"

"I think I will." Valeria fanned a hand in front of her face.

Akkon bent down and placed a small kiss to her lips before turning and heading in the direction of the drinks table. Those white robes he wore didn't hide his muscled frame. Instead, they only accented them. Those shoulders looked ready to bust the seams of his robes.

Managing to rip her eyes off of him, Valeria walked through an open set of double doors and into the cool night. Breathing in the fresh air, she smiled. She wished to see more of this planet. Was it necessary to her mission? No. But she found herself wanting to know Akkon more and to know him, she needed to know his people and the culture around her.

"I know what you're up to, human."

Valeria spun to find Zohx standing beside her. "Excuse me?" She asked even as her heart thundered in her chest. There was no way he knew why she was here and what her mission was. He was taking a shot in the dark… right?

Yet, if there was anyone out there who would find her secrets, she had no doubt it would be Zohx. He seemed like the sneaky snake type to her. She'd met several of his kind in her line of work, and they were never good news.

"And what might that be?" Valeria asked as she took a relaxed pose, leaning back against the balcony railing, keeping her arms loose beside her.

"You can't fool me." Zohx's eyes narrowed on

her. "A human who just happens to catch the eye of the king?" He snorted.

She shrugged.

"And he didn't even choose you."

Now that did surprise her. As far as she was aware, Akkon hadn't told anyone about her stealing away in his bathing pool. "Does it matter how we met?"

"A human who steals away to work her way into the king's heart?" Zohx snorted again as he leaned in closer, trying to intimidate her with his height. "I'm surprised you haven't killed him yet."

"Excuse me?"

"I'll bring you down before you harm him or any other Sri'thaen." Zohx took a couple of threatening steps forward.

"Zohx! I'll ask you to kindly step away from Valeria." Akkon's voice cracked like a whip.

Zohx shot backward as though a plasma stick had been pressed into his back. "As you wish." He inclined his head to Akkon. "Do be careful, my king. I fear you might have an assassin in your midst." He shot Valeria a withering look.

"Are you saying my judgment can't be trusted?" Akkon's voice leaked with venom as he growled each word.

Zohx inclined his head further. "I would never suggest anything like that."

"I think you should leave." It was less a suggestion and more an order. Wisely, Zohx spun around with a flutter of his robes and left them alone on the balcony as he strode back inside.

"Ugh, what is with him?" Valeria watched Zohx's back disappear into the crowd.

"Don't hate him too much. He has done good in my stead. And even if he wishes to be king, I can't find fault with him."

"And the war? How is that good for your people?" Valeria questioned.

Akkon's lips fell in a flat line. "War is never good. Must we get into it tonight?"

"No," she shook her head, "I'm sorry." Valeria waved a hand in the direction Zohx had disappeared. "He got my mind racing and got me all sorts of worked up."

A smile returned to Akkon's face. "Nevermind him. Zohx can't let anyone have a happy moment without finding some way to ruin it." He handed her one of the glasses he held.

"What's this?" She asked, and before he answered, she took a sip. It was bubbly and light, with a fruity tang that drew her back in for another sip.

"It's called *frifri*. It's a sweet alcoholic drink favored by anyone who can afford it."

"A drink of the upper class then?"

He nodded before he took a sip from his own glass. "What did Zohx have to say?"

Valeria sighed. Here she thought they weren't going to ruin the night with serious talk, but she also understood why he was curious. He probably wanted to reassure himself Zohx hadn't scared her away. "He seems to think I'm here to assassinate people."

Akkon arched an eyebrow. "And are you?"

Valeria sputtered on a sip of her drink. "You think the same?" A bit of hurt flooded her. Sure, she was here to do something, but she hoped he would give her the benefit of the doubt.

"No," Akkon said, "but you were the one who insisted I buy you." He prowled forward, crowding her up against the balcony railing. "It does sound suspicious."

"Or maybe," Valeria rocked her hips against him. A hard length prodded her from under his robes, and she tossed him a saucy grin. "Or maybe I simply wanted to make sure I got you rather than some nasty alien with sticky tentacles."

"I didn't realize," his head dipped to the juncture of her neck and shoulder, "I was the one on display that day." He pressed a kiss to her skin, sending a shiver of delight running through her. His hips ground into her, and she felt his length throb through his robes.

"Maybe we should find somewhere more private," Valeria said as she tilted her head, both giving him better access while sending a glance to the open balcony door. Anyone could step out and spot them, and she preferred to keep her sex life private.

With a snarl, Akkon nipped the skin on her neck. He pulled away with a glare to the open door. "You are right. It wouldn't do for someone to stumble upon us. Come." He grabbed her hand and pulled her down a set of stairs leading from the balcony to the grass below. He led her further into the palace gardens before finding a secluded area behind some thick bushes.

Before she knew it, he laid her out on the ground. His massive frame covering hers. The night sky glittered with the few stars that shone past the light pollution of the capital.

"How does this work for you?" Akkon asked as he nuzzled her neck.

"Much better. I've never done it out in the open before, so still a bit nervous."

Akkon chuckled. "Even if someone stumbles upon us out here, they won't be able to see clearly."

He had a point. It was extremely dark. She could barely make out Akkon above her.

"I thought palace gardens would be well lit at night."

"Hmm?"

Valeria smacked his shoulders until he pulled his head away from her neck. "Are you listening?"

"Not really," Akkon replied honestly. "Did I miss something important?"

"No."

"Good." He rose onto his knees and pulled his shirt up and over his head.

Even though she could barely make him out in the dark, Valeria reached up and stroked her hands down his chest. "Keeping this fit must take a lot of time out of your day."

"I exercise with our soldiers every few days."

"Maybe I could watch or even participate someday?" Valeria asked as her fingertips traced the ridges of his stomach.

"Whenever you would like to come, you need only ask."

A spark of desire shot through her. She wouldn't lie. Watching him fight and even kick another man's ass appealed to every single feminine fiber of her being.

"Take off your dress," Akkon commanded, his voice gone husky.

She disrobed, and after a couple fumbles with the zipper in the back, she wiggled out of the dress. When she glanced up, she saw he had done the same. The silhouette of his cock bobbing in the dark drew her attention. Valeria licked her lips as it drew her in like a moth to the flame. Wrapping a hand around it, she drew it to her mouth.

A groan above her let her know Akkon approved as she sucked the tip between her lips. She normally wasn't one to enjoy blowjobs, but she liked doing it for him. Which showed just how over her head she was. There was something in her heart that felt suspiciously like love. Their time may have been short, but it had been fun. More fun than she'd had with another man in a long time.

One of Akkon's hands landed on the back of her head. Gently. He guided her mouth up and down his cock.

"Mmmm." Valeria murmured.

Akkon sucked in a breath as the vibrations radiated around his cock like she'd hoped it would.

Every time her head bobbed up, she made it a point to run the tip of her tongue around the crown of his cock.

"Oh, Valeria." Akkon moaned. His fingers tightened in her hair, and then he pulled her head back.

Valeria pouted.

He chuckled in response. "If I let you continue sucking my cock, I would've spent myself in a matter of seconds."

"Kind of the point." She winked at him, not even sure he could see it in the dark.

"I'd rather be buried deep inside you when I come," Akkon growled back. He reached out, gripped her hips, and flipped her over. She landed on her hands and knees. Flipping her hair over one side, she turned her head to watch him. "Are you wet?"

"Why don't you find out?" Valeria wiggled her butt at him.

"I think I'll do just that."

His hand traveled up one of her thighs until he reached her hot juncture. Two of his fingers slid between her folds, and he groaned when he encountered the wetness there.

"What has you so hot?"

"Sucking your cock… and thinking about you kicking some ass in a training arena," Valeria said honestly.

Akkon smiled. "If just the thought turns you on this much, then I can only imagine how hot you'll be for me when I bring you to one of the training sessions."

His fingers slipped along her slick folds as he spread the wetness all around. When he encountered her nub, he rubbed a finger against it in tight circles.

Valeria's back arched into the air as she moaned and gasped. He loved how responsive she was to his lightest touch. Everything came so easily and naturally with her.

Slipping his fingers back through her folds, he found her entrance. The first and second fingers glided into her pussy with ease. His cock twitched in excitement as her tight pussy clenched around her fingers.

Her body trembled under him as he pumped his hand. She mewed and rocked her hips against his hand with every thrust. After a little bit, he withdrew his fingers. Lifting his hand towards her head, he commanded her, "Taste them."

With no hesitation, Valeria opened her mouth. He slipped the tip of his fingers into her mouth, and her lips closed down around them. Then her tongue swirled around his fingertips before she released them.

Akkon chuckled as his hands landed on her waist and held her steady. "Do you want my cock?"

"Yes." Valeria panted with a thrust of her hips.

"Needy woman."

"For you, yes. You've wound yourself around me." She admitted, and his heart stopped before thundering back to life at her words.

Grabbing a hold of his cock, Akkon positioned it at her entrance.

Valeria's eyes rolled back in her head as he thrust home inside her. His cock stretched her pussy wide. She moaned as his cock filled her, pressing against all her sensitive spots.

Once he gave her a moment, he grabbed her hair, yanking her back, forcing her to arch her back. The light pain on her scalp sent pleasurable sensations rolling through her. His hips moved, pumping his cock in and out of her in deep, quick thrusts.

Their gasps filled the cool night air. Light noises from the ball carried out to them, but no one inside would hear them.

Her fingers curled around the grass under her palms as she met his every thrust with her own. The wet slapping sounds of their sex and their pants were the only noises in her ears.

Then she felt him showering her naked back and shoulders with hot kisses as he continued pumping in and out of her. When he pulled out of her, she whimpered in need. Flipping her over, he laid across her and thrust his cock deep inside her.

Valeria's arms wrapped around his neck while her legs wrapped around his waist, her heels digging into his toned ass as she spurred him deeper. He rocked around her, his pumps now deep and fast.

"Yes. Yes." She panted as her head lolled to the side. His harsh breathing tickled the side of her neck. Soon her head thrashed against the grass as her body tightened before it finally exploded into sensation.

Akkon soon followed after her. With a grunt and then a groan, she felt his cock release his seed deep inside her, coating her pussy. His hips kept thrusting as they both rode every last wave of their desire.

Pulling free from her, he collapsed beside her on the grass. Reaching out, he drew her into his arms as they looked up at the dark sky above them.

"If you," Valeria said as she curled up against him, throwing a leg over one of his, "had told me I would fall for a Sri'thaen king, I never would have believed you."

Akkon laughed. "If you told me I would be king in all ways, I would have been intrigued but never believed you."

"Maybe we're good for each other."

"Maybe." He agreed, and his arms tightened around her briefly.

Chapter 11

"Good morning."

Valeria smiled as Akkon's breath tickled her cheek. It had been about a week since the ball, and she loved waking up next to him every morning. Stretching her arms above her head, she twisted around until she found him bracing himself on an elbow, slightly above her. "Good morning." She yawned.

"Did you sleep well?"

"I did."

A knock sounded on the door.

"Come in!" Akkon commanded the unseen person.

The door creaked open and a couple of servants filed in. They carried trays in their hands.

Grabbing the covers, she brought them over her chest as she sat up against the plush headboard. With a groan, Akkon did the same, and she didn't miss the bulge tenting the covers which anyone in the room would be able to spot.

One servant walked over to Akkon's side while the other came to Valeria's side of the bed. Valeria didn't miss the servant's gaze straying to Akkon's bulge. A sudden spike of anger flowed through her as the woman eyed it greedily. Sucking in a quiet breath, she quelled the jealous streak. Akkon wasn't hers, and he never would be. He was king of an alien species, and she was a spy who would be shot at dawn if anyone figured her out.

The servants drew back and then left the room.

Valeria glanced over her platter of food which laid across her lap supported by four legs, just like Akkon's tray. "Human food?" She eyed the pancakes and what looked to be bacon strips.

"I tasked some kitchen servants with finding and creating human dishes for you."

Valeria's heart swelled until she thought it might burst. This man was too much for her. Smiling, she leaned over and placed a kiss to his cheek. "Thank you for this. It means so much more than you know."

"I'm only sorry it took this long. The kitchen staff had to use Daen'su to get the human ingredients."

Daen'su. They were silver-haired, silver-eyed and basically ran the entire black market in space. If you needed it, they could and would find it… for a price.

Valeria took a bite of the pancakes. "Mmmm." She swallowed. "Pass along my compliments to the kitchen staff. Tastes perfect. Super fluffy. Heck, they are better than the ones from my childhood."

"I'll be sure the compliment is passed along." Akkon dug into his meal. "I thought we could go for another run today."

"Inside the castle grounds again?" Valeria felt certain they'd covered the extensive palace grounds thoroughly. She made quick work of the pancakes, nearly scarfing them down.

"I actually thought about bringing you out to a nearby forest. We will need guards to join us."

"Your protection or mine?"

"Both." Akkon frowned. "I won't pretend all my people are perfect. I'm sure there are a few out there who would take advantage of an unprotected king."

"No society is perfect. My people have a saying, the grass is always greener on the other side."

Akkon nodded his head. "It's a good saying."

"I am excited to see outside the palace walls." Valeria had been too many alien worlds to count. Normally they had a lot of similarities, but there were always slight differences, whether it be in the wildlife or the culture or just the looks of the aliens themselves. In some ways, her job was the best. It allowed her to explore and see things some people could only dream of at night.

"I think you'll enjoy the trails." Akkon moved his tray further down the bed, allowing him to slip out from under the covers.

Valeria's eyes skimmed up and down his body. The man was a god, not a king. It saddened her when she remembered he wasn't hers. All those sculpted perfect muscles would go to some other woman when she lost his attention or escaped the Sri'thaen home world. Because one day, she would leave. Either in a body bag or on a shuttle with a war fleet hot on her heels.

"Why has your face fallen?"

Blinking, Valeria realized he had dressed and turned to find her blindly staring at him. "No reason." She sent him a smile. "Just happy."

He frowned. "You didn't look happy. You looked like you might be thinking on something serious."

She moved the tray off to the side and sighed as she swung her legs over the edge of the bed. "It's hard not to wonder how long all this will last."

"What will last?" Akkon leaned up against a poster of the bed.

"Nothing." Valeria didn't want to get into it. Rushing over to the dresser, she pulled out some exercise clothing. The material was light-weight and airy without restricting any of her movements. It was nothing like she'd known before, and she would definitely steal a pair when she left.

"I will let it go then, but don't think I won't ask again," Akkon said from behind her.

"And I will tell you later when it won't ruin the fun of the day. I am excited," she turned around once dressed, "to see some more of your world."

"Then let me show you." Akkon held out a hand to her, and she didn't hesitate to slip hers into his waiting grasp.

When Akkon went off to participate in a fighting exercise, Valeria found herself feeling a bit lonely. She'd joined him for a few over the past few weeks, but she needed a rest right after running.

Her thoughts drifted to Sar, Fanka, and Alvae. She actually missed those three. It'd been a while since she last saw them now that she lived in Akkon's rooms. There'd been no reason for her to travel over to that side of the palace.

"Excuse me?" She glanced over to where a maid waited patiently in a corner.

The maid inclined her head as she stepped forward. "Yes, Mora?"

Valeria frowned. "My name is Valeria."

The maid inclined her head again, a patient smile on her lips. "Yes, Mora."

Well, she had tried. If the woman refused to use her name, there wasn't much she could do about it. "Umm, do you think I could visit the concubines?"

The maid's brow furrowed. "Why would you want to see them?"

"I became friends with them," Valeria explained. "I formed friendships with three of them." Or at the very least acquaintances. Maybe friends was too generous. It wasn't like any of them had shared super personal details about their family and such. She didn't even know Sar's favorite food. Still, they were more her friends than anyone else around.

"Would you like me to find you some more suitable friends, Mora?"

"Valeria." She corrected the maid again. "And no. I don't need you finding me more suitable friends. You can't find friends. You make friends."

The maid inclined her head. "I can take you to them."

"That would be perfect. Thank you." Valeria rose from her chair and rushed over, unable to contain her excitement. Waiting around for Akkon to come back was boring, and she wasn't really one for sitting around anyways. If she stayed here much longer, she needed a job or something.

The maid opened the door and then led the way down the hall.

Valeria didn't pay attention to her surroundings until she heard a voice dismiss her maid. Head snapping up, she gawked at Zohx storming up to her. Sucking in a steadying breath, she steeled herself. The maid scurried away like a fire burned at her heels.

"What is it with you humans?" Zohx pressed her up against a wall. "First a general, then a king, and now…" He trailed off as his eyes grew distant, almost like he thought about something else. Then they focused back in on her. "What is it with you?"

Valeria shrugged. Mainly, she had no idea how to answer his question. "We are spunky?" She tried.

"I feel myself needing more," Zohx muttered, and she knew she hadn't been meant to hear it. "How can one little human draw me in so much?"

Wait, what? Valeria blinked up at him. Raising her hands, she thrust him away from her. "I will not sleep with you, so don't even ask!" She hollered at him, ready to defend herself from any advances.

Zohx's face grew black as it scrunched up in horror. "You? You think I want you?" He pointed an accusing finger in her direction.

Valeria blinked. If he didn't refer to her, then did he know of another human who tempted him? "Do you know of another human?" The only ones she knew of were herself and Adira, a woman she had yet to meet but hoped to at some point. There were so many rumors running around about this woman. She sounded like an absolute badass, someone Valeria could see herself being friends with.

Instead of answering her, he whispered harshly, "Be careful where you tread, Valeria. I am searching for the captain of the slave vessel you arrived on, and when I do, I know he will have quite the tale to tell me."

A flicker of fear sent her heart skittering straight into her throat. As much as she wanted to believe the slave captain wouldn't reveal who she was, she knew there was only so much torture a person could take before breaking. "Try scaring someone else." Valeria's spine stiffened. "I have nothing to hide. You're simply envious of my position by the king's side."

She watched Zohx's fists clench and unclench by his sides. Oh, she knew he wanted to launch himself at her but also knew she still had the favor of the king. If he harmed her, Akkon would deliver swift justice.

"We will see what he says when my ship catches up to him."

She wasn't sure, but she thought Zohx might be threatening her. Did he already know where the captain was, and it was a matter of time? Or was Zohx trying to pressure her into a confession to save himself the trouble of all the work.

"Well, Zohx," she walked right up to him, placing her left shoulder at his right, "let's hope you're wrong about me being anything other than a sex slave, or you just put yourself on the top of my hit list." With that, she walked down the hall in search of her maid.

Chapter 12

The next couple of days were the most stressful of Valeria's life as she waited to hear what Zohx might turn up. Maybe it was time for her to cause some real chaos and get out fast. Then again, she still thought Zohx was simply pressuring her without evidence.

All this back and forth would cause her a stomach ulcer if she couldn't calm down.

"What are you thinking about?" Akkon asked as he traced a finger down her spine. She was sprawled out on the bed on her belly after another morning filled with passionate lovemaking.

"How fortunate I am to know you." Valeria sighed. It wasn't exactly what was on her mind, but it was true nonetheless.

"We are both fortunate then." Akkon kissed a trail down her spine. "Without you, the council would still be running the government on their own."

"Zohx would be running it." Valeria clarified.

"True," Akkon grunted as he rose from the bed and headed over to a dresser. He pulled out a white robe with gold trim.

"Have you thought any more about what I've said?"

"What was that?" He asked as he strode into the bathroom. She saw the flicker of blue light as he activated the sonic shower.

Valeria rose from the bed and walked over to

the bathroom door. Leaning against the frame, she said, "I know the Sri'thaen people think the war should still be brought to the humans, but what if you turned your attention less to the colonies and strictly to Earth government ships and planets?"

She was here to help Earth, but really, she just wanted to help those who were innocent in all this. She wanted to save lives. It was an Earth approved colony that started all this. Not all human colonies were supported or protected by Earth. Some made too little credits or didn't produce anything valuable enough for Earth government to care about them. Those colonies already struggled without the worry of a Sri'thaen warship coming into orbit and blasting them into non-existence.

"I have thought about what you said, and I think it makes sense. I don't think our mission should be to wipe out all humans. Instead, we should push Earth back to her borders and keep her there. Nothing more."

"So, you will bring it up to the councilors for today's lunch?"

"I will."

Relief swept through Valeria, and she walked away from the bathroom to seek out her own clothing. As she slipped into a nice day dress, she heard the door to the room open. When she turned, she saw a maid walk in. Akkon strode out of the bathroom clothed in his robes. The maid dipped into a curtsey before settling a tray of food on a table. As the maid turned to leave, her eyes caught on Valeria, and she dipped into another deep bow. "Please excuse me, Mora. I did not see you there, or I would have bowed sooner."

"It's fine." Valeria waved her concern away with a hand and a smile.

The maid scurried out the door, shutting it behind her with a click.

"Okay." Valeria tilted her head to the side as she studied the door. "What is it with these maids and not knowing my name?"

"Huh?" Akkon glanced over at her. He blinked several times. "What do you mean?"

She slipped the purple dress over her head. Picking at the fabric, she got it to roll over her hips. "I keep telling them my name is Valeria, yet they continue to call me Mora."

"Mora isn't a name. It's a title." Akkon chuckled as he slipped his feet into his shoes.

"What does it mean?" Valeria asked as she sat at the table and picked some food from the tray. There was nothing substantial, just some fruit, some more of that green cheese stuff she liked, and some crackers.

"I am Kelor, which means…" He thought about it before saying, "The closest translation would be king. And Mora means queen."

Valeria choked on a bite of her cheese. With tears pricking the corners of her eyes, she wiped at them as she asked, "Why do they think I'm a queen?"

"Would you like to be a queen?" He asked as he came to stand beside her.

"I, um, it's never been a dream of mine," Valeria said honestly. "When I was a kid, I always dreamed of being a ship mechanic like my father." Unfortunately, those math classes in college didn't go so well, so she chose another profession.

"What if I were to say you could be queen."

When she turned to stare up at him, he shrugged a shoulder as his eyes met hers. "My people already think you will be."

"But why do they think that? Have you given them any reason to believe I will be?"

"You moved into my chambers." Akkon sat down at the table and chose a couple of small fruits, popping them into his mouth.

"So…?"

Akkon pulled on the collar of his robe with a finger as he glanced away. "No king moves a woman into his chambers unless she will be the next queen."

Valeria blinked before she snapped. "When were you going to tell me this? It's not like I'm Sri'thaen. I didn't know when I moved in here I might be a queen." It also meant she would probably be watched more. Akkon always had guards lurking around him. Did that mean she had shadows following her that she hadn't noticed yet? Did Zohx have spies in place of the guards?

"I didn't realize it would anger you." He finally met her eyes.

If she was a sex slave, maybe she would be overjoyed. It would be the best thing to happen to her. Instead, it meant she might be stuck here with Zohx breathing down her neck. Being a queen wouldn't save her if Zohx brought proof of her being a spy. As she looked at Akkon she wondered if she should tell him, but fear froze her tongue.

Valeria couldn't say for certain how he would react to the news. "You want me to be queen?"

She swore a blush crept up his neck as he reached out and grasped one of her hands. "You're the first woman I've met who I imagined by my side. You've empowered me to take control of the councilors, helped me become a better man. A better king."

"I'm human." Valeria protested even as her heart bloomed under his words. He respected and trusted her enough to give her a position of power right beside him.

"Other than Zohx, has anyone made you feel unwelcome?" Akkon asked, his voice as cold as steel.

Well, there was the concubine posse that made her feel unwelcome, but she could handle those three women. Otherwise, none of the maids, guards, or councilors, other than Zohx, made her feel unwelcome.

"No. Other than Zohx I haven't been made to feel unwelcome here."

"Good." Akkon visibly relaxed at her words. "You should tell me if anyone ever does. I won't tolerate it from my people. Like you said, our war isn't with humanity. It's with Earth government."

"How do you think the councilors will take it?" Valeria asked, not intentionally switching the topic but also wanting more time to digest what she had learned. "How do you think they will take your new orders regarding the way the war is fought?"

"I think some of them will be agreeable, and some will oppose me," Akkon said truthfully.

"But your word can overpower them?"

Akkon nodded his head. "It does, but I'd like to have a majority on my side. I think it will look better to the people if it is a majority that agrees on this."

Valeria understood his reasoning. As much as she wanted to pressure him into making the decision without a majority, she knew she shouldn't. He needed his people to agree with him, to see him as reasonable, so she could continue to make changes in the background. Assuming she stayed long enough to do it. She still had Zohx waiting to pounce.

"We need to go and face the councilors at our lunch." Akkon smiled as he rose and offered her a hand. "Are you ready?"

"I was born ready." And she really was. As a kid, she could sneak anywhere and never get caught. She would snatch a slice of cake from the kitchen or steal another kid's toy without anyone being the wiser. "Show me the way."

"You're making a lot of changes." A female councilor complained. She rolled her beautiful blue eyes as she tossed her loose hair over one shoulder. Then her eyes landed on Valeria. "Some of us are wondering why."

"Because I was born to lead my people, and that means making decisions. Decisions some may not agree with." Akkon growled at her. "Seeking out every single human will be a drain on our resources. We might spend years, if not generations, attempting it. Instead, we should take our fight directly to Earth. Leave the unaffiliated colonies alone."

"I don't see why we can't do that." Another councilor spoke up. "It never sat right with me destroying these defenseless colonies."

Many of the councilors around the table

nodded their heads in agreement, but there were some who frowned.

As much as Valeria wished to chip in with her own words and opinions, she knew it would not be welcomed and might even hinder her efforts.

"The humans have always dared to overstep their bounds since flying into space. Should we not show them the errors of their ways?"

"Does that mean we have to destroy them?" Another councilor shot back.

Before she knew it, the whole room erupted into chaos. Councilors snapped at each other, and some even darted to their feet. Her mouth dropped open. She knew she'd been sent here to open a can of worms, but she didn't think the worms would be this easy to rile up.

Akkon reached over and grabbed her hand, squeezing it. When she glanced at him, he smiled. Smiled!

"Are you pleased with this?" Valeria asked, not even sure he heard her over the councilors yollering at each other.

"Actually, yes." Akkon's grin widened. "It's nice to see them finally voice their true opinions on the subject rather than saying what they think Zohx wants to hear."

With the mention of Zohx's name, Valeria searched him out at the table. He sat motionless watching the councilors. She wondered what he thought about all this. Was he taking notes on who agreed with him and who didn't?

As councilors calmed and seated themselves once more, Akkon rose.

"I value all of your opinions," he said as he spread his hands out in front of him, "but unless anyone can convince me differently, my decision stands. We will only attack Earth affiliated ships, space stations, planets, and colonies."

"What if we are fired upon first?"

"Then they will be fired upon as well," Akkon confirmed, and Valeria agreed with him.

"Looks like we didn't miss the lunch."

Valeria turned in her seat to see a human woman and a Sri'thaen general step into the room. This must be Adira and Rak. Adira looked like she was ready for war. She wore a space suit equipped with a couple of plasma pistols. Rak, on the other hand, was decked out in his formal robes.

"Please." Akkon motioned for them to sit at the table.

"Don't mind if I do," Adira said as she sat down and began loading up a plate with food.

"My apologies, Akkon. Adira has never been one to show any deference… at all." Rak said with a glower aimed at his wife, who already had a mouthful of food. But there was a gleam of pride and love in his eyes.

Akkon waved it away. "I have found out myself how much humans like to break rules." He glanced over at Valeria, and she smiled with a small shrug.

"My father raised me to be confident." She wouldn't apologize for her ability to stand up for herself, others, and what she wanted in life. It made her good at her job. There was no situation she couldn't handle.

"You've missed the king's new declaration," Zohx said, still seated at the table with his hands folded in front of him at the table.

"What's that?" Rak asked as he took a seat beside Adira. He laid an arm across the back of her chair.

"We are no longer hunting down just any human." Akkon sat back down in his seat. "From now on, our ships will only be allowed to fire on Earth affiliated ships, planets, space stations, and colonies. If we are fired on first, we will allow our men to fire back, of course."

Rak nodded his head. "I agree with this, and I know the other generals will agree. We prefer to fight soldiers than civilians."

Adira shrugged. "Whatever. My fight is with Earth, so as long as I get to cause them losses, I don't care."

"Slow down, or you'll choke." Rak grimaced as he watched his wife snarf her food. "You act like I starve you, woman."

"Don't judge me," Adira grumbled.

Valeria smiled as she watched them. They seemed perfect. Even from the other side of the table, she felt the love flowing off the both of them. She couldn't resist looking over at Akkon and wondering where they stood. She always felt her gaze drifting to him, and there was a suspicious ache in her chest when she thought about leaving or Zohx exposing her.

"Now, that is settled." Zohx rose as if reading her mind. When she met those icy eyes, he smiled. "May we talk about the spy in the room?"

Adira froze with a piece of sandwich posed at

her mouth. She glanced over at Zohx. "I thought all was forgotten and forgiven by now."

"It is," Rak growled as he looked ready to jump over the table to throttle Zohx.

"I'm not talking about you." Zohx smiled gleefully, and Valeria felt sweat gather at the back of her neck.

"What are you speaking of?" Akkon asked.

"Should I, or should you spill it?" Zohx asked, his gaze never leaving Valeria.

Instead of answering, she kept her mouth sealed. For all she knew, he had no evidence and only sought to scare her into a confession in front of everyone.

All eyes flew to her, and the bead of sweat grew into a puddle.

"Then I will say it."

"Wait," Akkon rose, "All other councilors will leave the room."

Mouths popped wide and eyes bulged.

"But…" One stammered.

"We should hear what Zohx has to say." Another said, "Especially if it has to do with this new human you call Mora."

Zohx's gaze turned to the king. "Mora?"

Valeria swore she heard Akkon's jaw pop under the pressure he exerted on it as he glared at Zohx.

"Out. Now." It was a command, and although new to his position, every councilor snapped to attention. Within moments the room was cleared, leaving only Akkon, Valeria, Zohx, Adira, and Rak.

"Should we leave?" Rak asked.

"No," Akkon said. "I might need someone to hold me back if I don't like what Zohx has to say."

Zohx didn't even flinch at the not so veiled threat. "I think Valeria is the one who will need protection. Not me."

"Spit it out already," Akkon growled as his hands wrapped around the table's edge.

Zohx tossed back one sleeve of his robes and pressed a button on the device on his wrist. The door to the room opened, and in walked the slave captain.

Valeria's stomach dropped to her feet, and she froze in her chair. He'd actually found the captain. She hadn't thought he would.

The captain met her gaze and sent her a wince. His face looked like one giant bruise, and she imagined under his clothing the rest of his body looked much the same. Zohx was one ruthless bastard.

"Who is this?" Adira asked, waving some sort of brown sausage with purple dots.

"This," Zohx said as he moved over to the captain's side, "is Captain Antonio. He," Zohx clapped an arm around the captain's shoulder, and the poor man flinched.

"So…?" Adira asked, seeming to be the only one interested in what Zohx had to say.

"He has some fascinating information about Valeria." Zohx continued. "Don't you?"

"I do." The captain croaked.

"Why don't you tell them?" Zohx coaxed.

"I was hired to bring Valeria here as a sex slave."

"Why did you do that?" Zohx prompted when the captain stopped.

"Because Earth wanted her to infiltrate the Sri'thaen government." Then he turned to meet Zohx's gaze. "But that's all I know."

"You may go," Zohx said as he moved away from the man.

Captain Antonio walked out of the room stiffly as though he couldn't move properly after his beating.

All eyes turned to her.

Valeria gulped. When she finally looked up at Akkon, she found him staring blankly at her.

"What is he saying?" Akkon finally asked.

"We should have left." Adira mumbled under her breath.

Rak shushed her.

"I… I was sent by Earth to infiltrate the Sri'thaen government. It is true." Valeria confirmed. "But that doesn't mean what we share means any less to me."

Akkon waved a hand, cutting off any more. "What were you to do?"

Sucking in a breath, she said honestly, "I was to assassinate or cause chaos among the Sri'thaen government. Earth didn't really care what I did, as long as I disrupted the war."

"As far as I know, you never assassinated anyone," Akkon said. "Unless you were biding your time to kill me."

"No." Valeria shook her head. "I would never harm you. Maybe at first, but when I got to know you better…"

"Stop." Akkon finally said after a few tense moments, "Please bring Valeria back to the concubine room and make sure she has a guard posted on her."

Zohx stepped forward. “Gladly.” Valeria felt her heart stop as Zohx’s hand wrapped around her bicep. As he led her away, he leaned into her ear and whispered, “I think you humans like to say, check mate.”

Chapter 13

Akkon stood there wondering what to do with himself. After the lunch, he'd planned on taking Valeria on a shuttle ride to visit the nearby cities around the capital. Mainly, he wanted to show off his Mora, his future queen. He wanted his people to love her as much as he did.

"I don't understand what the big deal is." Adira sighed as she placed the sausage on the table.

Akkon knew she wouldn't eat the sausage if she knew it came from giant cave spiders high in the mountains. Then again, Adira was a strange human and woman.

"Adira," Rak growled. "I'm sorry, Your Majesty."

"Explain," Akkon said as he slumped back into his seat.

Adira shrugged. "I'm just not sure what the problem is. Valeria is a spy, I was kind of a spy."

Rak snorted. "You were more than a spy. You were a force to be reckoned with."

Akkon agreed with that statement. "And your point?"

"Rak and I found a way to overcome our initial meeting. We were enemies turned lovers. Why can't you work it out with Valeria?"

Rak nodded his head. "Adira has a point. She kicked my ass a couple of times, but we managed to find a way to make it work."

"As much as I want to hope, I do worry it isn't quite the same." Akkon groaned as he placed his head in his hands. He didn't worry about showing Rak and Adira his indecision. He'd known Rak since childhood, and anyone Rak trusted, Akkon trusted. Which placed Adira in high regard.

"Anyone who sees you two together can see the love and admiration." Adira rolled her eyes. "We've only seen the two of you together for like thirty minutes, and I can tell she loves you. Maybe she came here on a mission, but she found more than just a target." Adira waved her hands at him. "Look at you, Akkon. You're king. Not just in title but in authority. She turned you from a caterpillar to a butterfly."

Both men frowned at her.

"Don't have butterflies?" Adira tapped a finger against her chin. "She made you a king." She shrugged. "I still don't know your analogies."

Rak murmured his agreement. "If she came to disrupt our government, then I think she failed. Now, I do think she completed her mission."

Akkon cocked his head. "How so?"

"She's helped some humans. Maybe not Earth, but she got you to agree to spare any human unaffiliated with Earth."

"Do you still agree with my decision?" Although Akkon wasn't so sure anymore that it was his decision. It had been Valeria's idea and his command.

"I do. We should take our war to Earth, not every human."

"It wasn't even my idea. It was Valeria's."

"Sounds like a king and queen working together to me." Adira raised a glass and toasted it high into the air. "We aren't saying make a decision on her right now. Think about it, but don't send her away either."

Rak nodded. "Again, I agree with Adira. Take some time. Let the hurt die down, and then revisit the matter. And whatever you do, don't let Zohx whisper in your ear."

"Thank you. I owe the both of you so much." There weren't many people he could turn to for help or guidance.

Adira and Rak both waved it away. "No, you don't owe us anything."

Akkon rose and wandered back to his rooms. The moment he entered, the silence and emptiness hit him.

Then his gaze landed on all her belongings. There were pieces of clothing strewn about. He supposed the maids had yet to come and clean.

Flopping onto the bed, Akkon immediately regretted his decision. Her delicate scent drifted up from her side of the bed. It filled his nostrils, and he groaned. Pushing up from the bed, Akkon left his rooms, searching for any place that didn't remind him of Valeria. He needed a moment alone without thoughts and memories of her bombarding him.

"Guess you didn't please the king as much as

you thought, Mora." Selde teased for about the fiftieth time.

"That's it. I'm killing you." Valeria jumped up from where she sat in the sunken lounge area.

Selde screamed in terror as she bolted away. Valeria followed hot on her trail. The woman's purple skin stood out starkly against the white of the concubine room.

Valeria gave the other woman credit when it came to running. Selde moved fast, just barely keeping out of Valeria's reach. Around and around they sprinted until Valeria finally zagged. Right as she almost cut off Selde, the guard who was stationed to watch her stepped into her path.

"There will be no harming the other concubines." He growled.

"She started it." Valeria pointed an accusatory finger in Selde's direction. The woman heaved in and out breaths as she glared back at Valeria.

"If you can't behave here, Zohx has given orders for you to be moved to a prison cell." The guard informed her.

Valeria scowled up at him. "Of course, Zohx did." She grumbled, but she turned her back to Selde and the guard. She strode back over to the sunken lounge and plopped down.

"Don't let her irritate you. She's still bitter you attracted Akkon's attention." Sar said with a scowl sent in Selde's direction. Then she turned back to Valeria. "When I heard you'd been moved to his rooms and people were calling you Mora, I was excited."

"No jealousy?"

"Not at all." Sar flicked a fuzzy off her dress

before scooting closer to Valeria. "Who wants to be queen with all the responsibilities it comes with? I'd much rather be a concubine sitting in luxury and no responsibilities. I don't even have to sleep with Akkon either. It's perfect for me."

Well, when Sar spelled it out like that, Valeria was inclined to agree. Except for the part about sleeping with Akkon. She liked sleeping with Akkon. Like waking up in his warm, strong arms.

"I think the tasks of a queen are part of the appeal for me," Valeria admitted. "I always enjoy a good challenge." And she loved being kept busy.

"The king hasn't packed you on a ship and sent you away, so I think there is still some hope for you becoming queen."

"Maybe he'll keep me here forever as punishment." Already two full days had passed since her secret was revealed. Zohx had yet to get her shot at dawn, but he had wrecked her budding relationship with Akkon.

"Or he needs time," Alvae commented from her seat, where she busied herself with a small device that colored her toe nails. As the device whirred to life, she looked up. "He thought he knew you. A woman he saved from being a sex slave, and now he's found out you're not as helpless as he first thought. He needs time to process and realize you're not here to harm him. You helped him."

"And he's a fool if he doesn't realize it." Sar chipped in. "That man wasted his life and kingship away until you showed up."

Valeria hoped he realized she may have come here to complete a mission, but she wanted to stay because he'd penetrated her heart. Now she feared he'd cast her aside and shatter it. Then again, perhaps she shouldn't blame him for a possible broken heart. Maybe if she had been honest sooner things would have been different.

Ugh. She wasn't going to do that to herself. She couldn't keep wondering what could and would have happened had she done something differently. She acted, and she couldn't take it back.

With a huff, Valeria leaned back against the soft cushion and closed her eyes. At least Akkon wasn't sending her to the firing squad. Not every king would be so lenient.

"Valeria."

Freezing, Valeria didn't believe her ears when she heard Akkon's voice call out to her. She opened her eyes to find Sar and Alvae gazing over her head. Turning in her seat, she glanced up and out of the sunken lounge to see Akkon standing in front of her. She rose, nearly tumbling over her own feet in her rush. Her heart pitter pattered around inside her chest.

"Akkon."

"Can we speak? Privately?" He asked as his eyes skimmed over the women sitting behind her.

"Of course." Valeria felt her heart tumble around in her chest as she walked up the couple of stairs.

Akkon placed a hand on the small of her back and guided her out of the room. When the guard moved to follow them, Akkon dismissed the man with a hand movement.

Once alone as they walked through the palace halls, she asked, "What would you like to talk about?"

"Not here," Akkon said as he guided her further down the hall. He led her up to a set of double doors. Stepping in front of her, he braced his hands on the doors and swung them open.

Valeria's breath left her as she stepped onto the balcony. The night sky spread out above her, and below she got a splendid view of the lit up city. The city lights blocked the light of the stars, but the city twinkled just as delightfully.

"What is this?" Valeria asked as she spun around. She gasped again when she found Akkon kneeling in front of her. He held a small black box in his hands.

"What…?"

"Adira was kind enough to tell me how humans propose, and," Akkon shrugged with a smile, "I think this is much more romantic than Sri'thaen ways." With that, he opened the black box.

Valeria's eyes fixated on the ring. The center stone was a gleaming purple gem surrounded by gold decorative swirls. "It's pretty."

"Will you be my Mora? My queen?"

Valeria nodded, her heart soaring into the sky as she held out a hand. "I might ask you to pinch me later."

"Why would you do that?" He asked as he slipped the ring onto her finger.

"Because this might be a dream. Humans believe a pinch can wake them from a dream."

Akkon rose and drew her into his arms.

Valeria placed her hand on his chest and admired the ring. "I never thought I would ever see a ring on my finger. My job makes me a lot of enemies and not many suitors."

Akkon chuckled. "I'm afraid you'll have to give up being an assassin and spy. Instead, you will have to become a queen and focus on your people."

"Oh," she glanced up at him, "I think being queen will give me plenty of challenges." The smile grew on her face. "Have you told Zohx yet?"

"Let's not try to irritate him, shall we?" Akkon rolled his eyes with a sigh.

Valeria pouted. "But it's so much fun." Especially now, when she had Akkon back on her side. Zohx tried to get rid of her, but he failed.

"I know." Akkon leaned down and placed a kiss to her mouth. "I did tell the councilors I would be keeping you here as my queen, but Zohx was occupied. Some of the councilors are upset with my decision, and some are fine with you becoming queen."

"What's the percentage okay with it?" Valeria asked.

"Maybe twenty percent."

Valeria snorted. "Not many then."

"It won't be easy," Akkon admitted. "It will take them time to grow used to a human as queen."

"What do they protest more? Me being human or how I came to be here? Ouch!" Valeria drew back slightly in Akkon's arms when he pinched her backside. "What was that for?"

"Just reminding you it's not a dream, and we will find a way past all and any obstacles."

Akkon unwrapped his arms around her and guided her to a small table with two chairs. They took their seats, and it was only then she noticed the plates of food.

"Looks good."

"These are traditional dishes. I thought you might enjoy them."

"I'm always ready for something new." Valeria eagerly tucked in before he had a chance to explain the food laid out before her. "So," she said between bites, "what do they protest more?"

Akkon didn't even need to take a moment. "They protest a human queen."

"I thought so."

He cocked an eyebrow.

"They seem to welcome Adira, and she's only been here a couple of months. I figured it's because she wasn't offered the position of queen."

"Like I said, it won't be easy."

"I don't like easy. I like challenges."

Epilogue

"What if we don't want jobs?" Selde asked as she folded her purple arms in front of her chest. She sent a death glare straight at Valeria.

"Then we will find you somewhere else to live while the king provides a modest lifestyle for you. There will be no luxuries, just what you need to survive. Enough money for basic necessities." Valeria said as her eyes skimmed over the concubines in front of her.

"The king is offering to pay for us to learn skills and get jobs?" Sar asked.

"Yes." Valeria smiled at them all. "It was my idea. I figured most of you would be okay with this." And Valeria wasn't keen on marrying a man with concubines, even if he didn't sleep with any of them. "Akkon agreed there was no more use for concubines. He wants you to be able to marry, have children, and start your life."

"This is exciting!" Fanka clapped her hands together.

"A little scary, but, yes, it is exciting." Alvae agreed.

"You won't be kicked out of the palace any time soon." Valeria rushed to reassure them. "We, of course, understand you all will need time to decide which path you want to take with your life."

"What if we would like to remain a

concubine?" Sar asked, which surprised Valeria a little. She always assumed the other woman would jump at the chance to do something else.

"I can talk to Akkon about looking for other Sri'thaen men who would like another concubine. You can meet them and decide which to choose. We are up to ideas, so feel free to let me know."

The women nodded and dispersed. A few looked happy about it and some not so much. With a sigh, she left the room and went in search of Akkon. She found him training with his men in an arena. When he noticed her, she broke off from the men.

"How did it go with the women?" Akkon asked as he set down a pole. They used these poles to attack and defend themselves during their training. She'd been whacked a couple of times on her butt by Akkon when he trained her. She swore she could still feel the sting.

"Okay. I think they need time to get used to the idea. Some even want to remain in a harem."

"I am sure I can find some suitable men who would want them." Akkon drew her into his sweaty arms. "In the meantime, let's get cleaned up before the wedding planner arrives. She's never done a wedding as elaborate as a human wedding, but she's up for the challenge."

"My kind of woman." Valeria chuckled as they headed for his bathing pool.

www.ingramcontent.com/pod-product-compliance
Ingram Content Group UK Ltd.
Pitfield, Milton Keynes, MK11 3LW, UK
UKHW042017190726
13854UKWH00005B/2336

9 798476 646600